Lady in Waiting . . .

Tom climbed into bed while Louise undressed. She enjoyed disrobing in front of an appreciative man. And Tom was that, she could see. His eyes roamed over her flesh, taking in the soft swell of her breasts and then moving down to the flaring hips and thatch of curly pubic hair. He was already getting hard, she noted with satisfaction. She started to turn down the lamp, then decided against it, wanting to enjoy the sight as well as the feel of his hard-muscled body.

Then, climbing in beside him, she let her slender fingers tangle in the mass of dark hair on his chest as the vibrations of warm passion surged through them both. "I want you," she whispered, her lips half parted, her eyes glimmering with lust. "I want everything you've got . . . I want you to make love to me like you've never made love to any other woman."

Her hand moved down between his lean thighs where his manhood was now hard and throbbing, teasing it with her nimble fingers until he was in a frenzy of lust.

She gave a cry of joy as he pushed her down on her back. Her thighs squeezed provocatively around his hand in a lewdly inviting caress. "Now," she pleaded. "Oh, God, don't make me wait!"

BRIAN O'NEILL

CAVENAUGH'S REVENGE

PINNACLE BOOKS NEW YORK

This is a work of fiction. All the characters and events portrayed in this book are fictional, and any resemblance to real people or incidents is purely coincidental.

CAVENAUGH'S REVENGE

An original Pinnacle Books edition, published for the first time anywhere.

First printing, March 1982

ISBN: 0-523-41637-7

Cover illustration by Earl Norem

Printed in the United States of America

PINNACLE BOOKS, INC.
1430 Broadway
New York, New York 10018

Chapter One

It had been a long, tiring ride up from Tombstone, and U. S. Marshal Tom Cavenaugh's big bay gelding, sensing food, water, and rest ahead, whinnied with excitement and picked up the pace as it sighted the sun-baked settlement of Whitehorse Junction shimmering in the desert heat a mile or so off in the distance.

The lawman gave his animal its head, hunching forward in the worn saddle and adjusting his lean body to the increased speed. He rode effortlessly, almost like an Indian, wasting no energy, letting his horse do the work.

Tom was a tall man of thirty-four years, hard-muscled and trim under the dusty trail clothing he wore. Not a particularly handsome man, he had, nevertheless, the kind of rugged features which looked as if they had been sculptured from mountain granite, and which most females found both intriguing and attractive—especially the long crease of hardened white scar tissue which ran across his forehead from temple to temple in stark contrast to the surrounding tanned flesh. The scar was an old wound, a souvenir from a gunfight years before when his scalp had been laid open by a drunken Mexican's bullet in Tucson. The scar was a constant reminder to the lawman of how capricious fate could be: Had the Mexican's aim been only a fraction of an inch more accurate, Tom would have died on the spot, with splinters of his skull exploding into the pulpy mass of his brain. Instead, something had distracted the Mexican and he had died in the dusty street instead of Tom. Over the years Tom had acquired the habit of stroking the scar for luck whenever he was called upon to face another man down. More than once the gesture had disconcerted his opponent, giving Tom a split-second advantage.

Not that he often needed any advantage.

Tom Cavenaugh was a hard case, as quick with his guns and his fists as any man in the territory. There were few so stupid as to want to provoke him into violence and, when some fool did, it was usually a fatal mistake for that party. Tom tried to avoid such confrontations when he could reasonably do so, but he had long ago learned that turning the other cheek was a dictum that could come back to haunt a man in his profession.

He gently reined in his horse now as they rode into the dreary desert settlement. He had not been in Whitehorse Junction for years, but he could see that it had changed but little, and only for the worse. The settlement was a motley collection of crumbling adobe buildings, interspersed with weather-worn frame structures of more recent age. Years before, when Arizona was still a part of Mexico, the settlement had been a thriving rancho. Now it was just a backwater stage station and supply point for the prospectors who prowled the surrounding mountains in search of gold and silver. Years before there had been some speculation that the north-south railway line would come through Whitehorse Junction, and there had been something of a boom as speculators rushed in to buy up land. Then, when the territorial capital had been moved up to Prescott from Tucson in 1877, everyone knew that the railroad line would be fifty miles to the west of Whitehorse, and those of its citizens with any ambition or sense had moved on.

It was almost four o'clock as the horse and rider moved up the single street toward the combination stage-and-livery stable. The sun would disappear behind the mountains before long, but it was still blazing hot, and even the mangy street dogs refused to leave the shade of their sheltered dens to investigate this stranger, sensible enough to let him pass with only an indifferent growl.

As he eased off his horse in front of the stable, Tom Cavenaugh thought about the wire which had summoned him from his permanent assignment in Tombstone to this godforsaken spot almost the length of the territory. The wire ordering him to Whitehorse Junction had come in over the army telegraph to Fort Huachuca the week before. Since Tombstone was not yet on the military communications system, an army dispatch rider had delivered the message to Tom the following day. Signed by Aaron Mason, chief U. S. marshal for the territory, the wire had originated in Prescott. Tom was to drop whatever he was doing and meet U. S. Marshal Amos Wicklund in Whitehorse Junction on urgent, if unexplained, business. Wicklund would provide all the details, according to the wire.

Tom had done as ordered, leaving Tombstone immediately, looking forward to seeing his old friend Amos Wicklund again. The two men had served along the Mexican border years before when Tom was a green recruit, Amos already a hardened veteran of the U. S. marshals' force. Although they had not seen one another in several years, their friendship was not the type to be diminished by time or distance.

He took off his Stetson and wiped his sweaty forehead with the sleeve of his faded denim shirt as his horse quickly headed for the nearby water trough. Suddenly Tom looked up as a voice greeted him from the darkness of the stable.

"Howdy, mister," a middle-aged, balding man said. "Come on in out of the sun, for God's sake."

When Tom was inside the cool building, the man extended a beefy hand and introduced himself, eyeing the silver badge on Tom's vest. "I'm George McBain, the manager of the stage station. And you'd be Marshal Cavenaugh, I suppose."

"I am," Tom replied, shaking hands. "I'm supposed to meet Amos Wicklund here. Has he arrived?"

"Yes, he came in three days ago, but he rode out last night to check on some stray Indians over by Sweetwater. He'll be back tonight or tomorrow morning at the latest, he told me to tell you."

Tom was disappointed that his old friend wasn't there to greet him, but it would give him a welcome chance to clean up and catch a few hours of sleep before Amos arrived. He turned as his horse came into the stable and nudged him impatiently, anxious to be rid of the saddle and tack. Before Tom could do so, McBain relieved him of that chore.

"Let me do that, Marshal Cavenaugh," he said quickly. "Why don't you go on inside and try some of my old woman's venison stew. Then she can fix you up with a bath and a bed for the night. There ain't a hell of a lot of excitement here in Whitehorse, I'm afraid, but you'll find the grub tasty and the bed'll be clean."

"A good feed and a night's rest will be excitement enough for me," Tom grinned. He started out of the stable, but the older man stopped him.

"Did you come up through Tucson and Phoenix?" he asked. When Tom replied that he had, the other man went on, coloring slightly with embarrassment. "Is it true what folks tell me about them new whorehouses down there? That them fancy ladies can turn a young man old overnight with all the tricks they know to please a man?"

"Don't believe everything you hear, Mr. McBain," Tom laughed. "Most of the whores I've met are either fat, ugly, or dirty . . . sometimes all three. They know some tricks, all right, but it's usually how to give a man a dose of the cock-rot or to steal his money while he's rolling around in bed. Why do you ask, Mr. McBain?"

The older man was more embarrassed than ever.

"Ah, you know how it is," he replied sadly, shaking his greying head. "Living in a shit-hole like this gives a man more time than's good for him to think about foolishness like that. But, damn it, I sure as hell would like to spend a week with one of them fancy ladies before I croak out here in this godforsaken desert!"

Tom nodded sympathetically. He guessed McBain's age to be sixty, but the man looked older. It was always a dangerous time for a man that age, living in a place like Whitehorse Junction, facing nothing but old age and continued boredom. A man's thoughts would naturally focus on things he wanted but didn't have. Well, Tom thought sadly, fifteen minutes with a smelly, overweight whore would quickly make McBain appreciate the things he *did* have.

The lawman smiled and turned to leave again, asking, "Am I your only guest tonight?"

"Yeh, you sure are," McBain told him. "Hell, son, there's only about twenty of us in the whole damned settlement. And there's just me, my old woman, my hired hand Caleb, and the girl who helps my missus." He paused, then went on. "I'd better tell you about the girl, I guess. Her name's Margo, and she's a little odd up here." He paused again, tapping his head with a stubby forefinger. "Not that I blame her, of course, seeing what she went through."

"You mean she's crazy?" Tom asked.

"Well, kinda touched, if you know what I mean. She and her folks had a small farm over in Kilroy, you know, Mormons. Anyway, a bunch of renegade Apaches killed her folks and kidnapped Margo when she was just barely sixteen. The bastards treated her pretty badly, I guess, before an army patrol found her wandering around in the mountains last year. She'd been with the Indians for almost two years. That ain't the worst of it, though. A couple of Indians got to fighting over who was going to sleep with the girl and the one who lost figured he'd fix her so nobody would want her. He carved up her face pretty bad with a knife. She must have been purty thing before it happened, but she's a scary sight now with her face like that."

The story was a familiar one, even though most of the Indians were quiet enough now, except for a few renegades who continued their sporadic raids on farms and ranches. The practice of taking white women and children to use as whores and slaves had died out, for the most part, however, when the Indians realized that nothing was as certain to bring the wrath of the army and settlers down on them. Still, it happened in isolated instances. And God help the captives!

"How'd the girl end up here?" Tom asked quietly.

"Well, she was too ashamed to want to go back to the Mormons," McBain replied bitterly. "No man would want her and she'd be treated like an outcast by the other women. She stayed at the army hospital in Fort Verde for a few months, then one of the sergeants and his missus took her in and made a goddamned slave out of Margo . . . working her from sunup to sundown and barely giving her enough to eat, by Jesus! And that ain't the worst. The sergeant's old woman was jealous of the girl and her husband, and she treated Margo worse than she would have treated a damned squaw. The girl ran off a couple of months ago and I found her out here in the stable one morning, half-crazy from hunger and fear. We been looking after her ever since but, like I said, she ain't right in the head yet, and she runs and hides every time a man looks at her . . . which ain't often, because she sure don't like to show that cut-up face of hers. I'm only telling you this so you won't be surprised when you see her."

"Don't worry, Mr. McBain, I'm not going to embarrass the girl," Tom replied, getting the point.

"I didn't figure you would, Marshal Cavenaugh,"

McBain went on. "But it ain't easy to look at her without reacting to how she looks. Hell, I ain't used to it *myself*, if you know what I mean."

Tom thanked the station manager and crossed the yard to the main building. It was a long, low adobe structure—probably the rancho's original *casa*, he guessed. Inside, what had been the main parlor had been turned into a dining room and bar. Several communal dining tables sat empty. A door opened off the left wall into the kitchen and to the right was a passageway which led to the McBain's quarters and the rooms for overnight guests.

Tom hung his Stetson and gun on the hat-rack and strode over to the kitchen door. The delicious aroma of bubbling venison stew wafted out at him, making his hunger acute. A plump, red-faced, older woman stood at a table making biscuits, while a young female—her back to Tom—washed dishes in the sink.

"Hello," Tom called out. "Any chance of getting some of that stew?"

The older woman looked up, smiling broadly. The girl at the sink jerked her head around and stared at Tom for a split-second, then looked away again before he could see her face. From the back she looked very young. Tall and slender, her long dark hair hung almost to her waist.

"You must be Marshal Cavenaugh," Mrs. McBain said, wiping her hands on her apron as she came toward Tom. "Amos Wicklund has been telling us what a handsome devil you were, son, and I thought he was lying, like he always does." She paused, grinning at him as she looked him over. "Kind of thin, though," she went on. "You grab a seat and we'll put some meat on those bones of yours."

Tom liked the woman immediately. He smiled back and sat down at one of the tables. In a moment she was back with a heaping plate of steaming, savory-smelling stew and biscuits. "You dig into that, son, and then I'll get you more if you're still hungry."

She sat down across the table from the lawman and watched him wolf down the food. It was Tom's first real meal since Phoenix, and it was delicious. When he congratulated Mrs. McBain between bites, she shrugged off the compliment and called out for the girl in the kitchen to bring Tom coffee.

"I love to see a man eat," she laughed. "I can see you don't have a woman of your own to keep you fat and sassy, son. Well, we'll put a few pounds on you while you're here. Did my husband tell you Amos had to ride over to Sweetwater after some Indians who've been rustling cattle? He's sure looking forward to seeing you, son. Mind, he's been a touch preoccupied about something, not funning like he usually is and making up to me. I suppose it's something to do with why you're here, son. He wouldn't tell me or Mr. McBain what it was about." She paused again, looking toward the kitchen. "Margo! You get out here with that coffee. This poor man is waiting, girl!"

Looking back at Tom, she lowered her voice.

"Did Mr. McBain mention Margo?" she asked in a whisper. When Tom indicated he knew about the girl, Mrs. McBain went on. "Poor thing. She's dead bashful about strangers seeing her. Please don't stare at her face, son."

Before Tom could answer he heard footsteps behind him, then saw the girl's slender arm reach around his back to set a large mug of steaming coffee on the table. "Margo, say hello to Marshal Cavenaugh," Mrs. McBain called out to the girl. "Marshal, this is Margo."

The girl mumbled something incoherent as Tom looked around at her. He purposefully kept his eyes lowered, but he couldn't miss the ugly red scar that had turned the girl's otherwise pretty face into something grotesque. The scar had been slashed from the left cheekbone down across her nose and ended on the right side of her chin. With good medical attention at the time of the wound, the thing might have been less ghastly. Unfortunately, the deep knife cut had been treated only with ground fire ashes and herbs, and had healed imperfectly, with the ingrained ashes leaving the scar tissue black and ugly. The girl, sensing Tom's shock, colored deeply and then swung around and quickly fled the room.

"Jesus!" Tom gasped.

"Ain't it awful?" Mrs. McBain said bitterly. "It was bad enough seeing her folks killed by the Indians and then having them use her like they did! But, God, to have one of them mar her like that! And then to be treated so badly by all the so-called *decent* people since! I swear, son, the preachers can talk all they want about Christian *charity*, but I've not seen much of it in my days. And, if folks aren't making faces at the poor little thing and laughing at her, they're acting as if she *wanted* to be taken captive by the Indians or, even worse, as if she should have killed herself after they did those horrible things to her!"

Tom's appetite was suddenly gone and he pushed away his plate. What a waste, he thought bitterly. The girl Margo—*any* girl, for that matter—deserved better than the kind of treatment she had received, first at the hands of the savages, then from the whites who were at least as cruel in a different way. Thank God for people like the McBains, he told himself.

"I'd sure appreciate a bath now," he said, pushing his chair away from the table and standing up. "Can you fix me up?"

"You just come with me, son," she replied, leading him out through the kitchen. Margo didn't look up from the sink when they went out the kitchen door and to a small frame structure behind the main house. A barrel of water rested on the roof, with a connecting iron pipe feeding the sun-warmed water into a zinc-lined tub inside.

"You have a good soak," Mrs. McBain said solicitously, laying clean towels on the stool beside the tub. "Just throw your dirty clothes outside and I'll wash them for you."

When she had gone, Tom undressed and got into the tub, groaning with pleasure as the warm water eased his aching muscles and cleansed the trail dust off his body. The water felt so good that he filled his pipe and lit up, puffing while he soaked. Suddenly he was alert as he heard the sound of a horse riding up to the stable. Thinking it might be Amos Wicklund, he quickly completed his bath and toweled himself dry, then put on the clean clothing from his saddlebag. He needed a shave, but that would have to wait, he decided, anxious to see Amos.

He was just putting on his boots when he heard footsteps running toward the bathhouse. "Marshal! Please, come quick!"

It was obviously the voice of the girl Margo.

"What's up?" Tom called out, throwing open the door, alarmed by the sense of urgency and fear in the girl's words. She was standing a few feet away from the bathhouse, wringing her hands, her scarred face contorted with fright.

"What's the matter, girl?" Tom asked, moving toward her.

"It's Sergeant Callahan . . . he's going to hurt Mr. McBain! Oh, please, don't let him do anything to them!"

She turned and ran back toward the house. Tom followed as quickly as he could, pulling on his boot as he ran. Margo raced into the kitchen and stopped at the doorway that led into the dining room, too frightened to go any further.

"In there!" she cried out in a hoarse whisper, pointing into the other room. "Please, don't let him hurt them!"

Tom had no time to ask the girl who Sergeant Callahan was. Brushing her aside, he moved quickly into the dining room. The station manager and his wife were standing together behind the bar, their faces ashen, either from fear or anger. Tom couldn't decide which, but he could see why they were upset. A hulking, heavy-set man well over six feet tall, dressed in an army cavalryman's uniform, stood in front of them, his back to Tom.

"Damn it, McBain, I know the little slut is here," the soldier said harshly, still unaware of Tom's presence. "You get her out here right now . . . I want to talk to her!"

"Well, by Christ, she don't want to talk to you, Sergeant Callahan!" McBain replied hotly. "Margo told us how you and your woman treated her up at Fort Verde . . . working her like a slave and your wife making fun of that scar on Margo's face. No, sir, by God, I won't have you bothering her. Go on, get out of here. I don't want your kind stinking up my place!"

"I'll have none of your sass, you old fucker!" the soldier roared angrily. "Did the whore tell you she owed us three month's board for her food and her keep? Me and my missus took the bitch in when nobody else would, and I aim to get my money."

"You'll get *nothing* from her!" Mrs. McBain cried out. "Leave us alone!"

The soldier reached for McBain's shirtfront, grabbing it and pulling the station manager toward him. Tom reacted quickly. "Hold up there, soldier!" he commanded, moving across the room. Surprised by Tom's voice, Callahan spun around and stared incredulously at the lawman. His forage cap was pushed back on his shaven head and rivulets of sweat poured down over his face. His features were gross and menacing, from the broken nose to the fat lips which curled back to reveal yellowing teeth.

"Who in the fuck are *you*, mister?" he demanded in a sneer. There was no fear in his eyes, only irritation at being distracted. He made no move toward the holstered colt revolver strapped to his middle.

"The name's Cavenaugh," Tom said coldly, "U. S. *Marshal* Cavenaugh. You'd better tell me why you're threatening a man half your size and twice your age."

"This is army business, mister," Callahan said sarcastically. "These two old fools are harboring a girl who ran off owing me and my missus fifteen dollars board money. We was good hearted enough to take the bitch in when nobody else would. We fed her and give her a place to sleep and that's how she paid us back . . . by running off. I aim either to get the money or take her back so she can work it off."

"Margo *worked* for anything she ever got from you!" Mrs. McBain interrupted. "You're not taking her anywhere!"

Tom didn't have to know any of the details to understand now what the problem was. If was common practice on army posts that the senior noncom's wife had first call on any laundry or cleaning work done for the officers or civilians. It was a lucrative trade, and most of them employed other wives, half-breeds, widows, and younger girls to do the actual work while they collected the fees. It was pure drudgery and little money for anyone unlucky enough to need that kind of work. Clearly, the sergeant and his wife had not been motivated by any humanitarian spirit when they took Margo in.

"Did the girl work for your wife?" Tom asked.

"Yeh, but she was too damned lazy to earn her keep," Callahan scoffed. "My wife even had to take a stick to her skinny ass to get her to do anything at all. But this is none of your business, mister."

He started to turn toward the McBain's again when Tom grabbed his arm and stopped him. "I'm making it my business," he said. "If you've got a complaint against the girl you take it to a magistrate. She's not in the army and this isn't Fort Verde, so you'd best get on your horse and hightail it out of here, soldier. My advice to you is not to come back or bother these folks . . . or the girl, again."

"Keep your goddamned advice," Callahan screamed, spraying Tom with his fetid spittle. Suddenly he caught sight of Margo in the kitchen doorway and his rage increased. "Get out here, you dirty little injun fucker! Come on, bitch, settle up what you owe me and my missus. Damn, I'd almost forgotten what an ugly whore with that injun's knife mark on you! I'm hanged if I know how anybody can stand to look at you without puking!"

He started toward the girl, grunting with pig-like laughter at his own wit.

Any weariness Tom had felt was gone in an instant as he raced after Sergeant Callahan. He managed to get between the soldier and the girl, balling his fist and ordering the man to stop. Callahan ignored Tom, trying to shove him aside, yanking at the flap of his holster while Tom struggled to maintain his footing.

Tom's own gun was still on the rack, twenty-odd feet away from where he stood. He knew his only chance was to disarm Callahan before the man could fire. All right, you bastard! he thought, dropping to one knee and driving his fist as hard as he could into the sergeant's middle. There was a sudden explosion of rage and pain as Callahan doubled over. He tried to bring the gun up and point it at Tom, but the lawman grabbed the cold steel of the barrel and held it tightly with his left hand while he used the hard heel of his right to smash into the sergeant's forearm. The man's bone broke with an eerie crack and then there were more shrieks of agony. But instead of letting go of the gun, Callahan's fingers clutched it more tightly.

"Drop it, goddamn you," Tom shouted, jumping to his feet again while he tried to dislodge the revolver from the soldier's hand. It was no use. The more he tried, the harder Callahan fought. Very few men could take such pain, Tom knew, and he realized he would have to bring the sergeant down quickly before the gun went off and a wild shot jeopardized the girl or the McBains. Margo seemed frozen in the doorway, unable to move, as were the station manager and his wife.

Tom balled his fist again, this time driving it brutally against the soldier's nose and mouth. A startled, inhuman expression flashed across Callahan's face, then his mouth opened and blood and gore splattered against Tom's shirt. Then Tom was aware of a searing pain in the hand that held the gun barrel as a loud explosion rocked the room. He looked down, seeing a wisp of oily smoke coming from the barrel, and he could hold it no longer. His burning fingers came away at the same time as Callahan groaned in misery and let the weapon slip from his fingers.

Enraged, Tom brought his fist up again and punched the soldier in the face with two lightning-like blows that drove Callahan to the floor. The sergeant tried to say something, but nothing came from the mangled lips but the mushy sound his tongue made against the blood that filled his mouth. He wasn't finished yet, however. With a desperation born of the incredible pain he felt, Sergeant Callahan used his good left hand to reach down and snake out the bowie knife from his dusty boot, struggling at the same time to sit up.

Tom watched in horror as the knife was drawn backwards, held by the tip, aimed at his body. Then, suddenly, he came to his senses and reacted. Bracing himself, he leaped in the air and jumped forward at the same time. The heels of his boots landed squarely on Callahan's chest. The strangled sound that flew from the soldier's lips was like nothing Tom had ever heard before. It started low, then built, ending in a tortured scream of unearthly agony. The knife had dropped to the floor, skidding out of Callahan's reach. Unable to keep his balance, Tom fell heavily beside the sergeant, rolling away, then coming up to his knees.

But it was over.

Callahan's body lay in a tangled heap, his limbs askew, his broken arm flopping about helplessly in the sawdust, blood streaming from his nose and mouth.

"Jesus H. Christ!" McBain gasped, coming over to kneel beside the soldier. "You've killed the bastard, son."

"He's not dead," Tom moaned, watching Callahan's chest rise and fall as the man struggled for breath. "He's going to need a doctor, though. I don't suppose there's one in town, is there?"

"In Whitehorse?" McBain scoffed. "We'd best throw him in a wagon and send him over to the hospital in Prescott. I don't know that he'll live that long, but it's the only chance he's got."

McBain's wife had gone into the kitchen to look after Margo. Her husband shouted for her to fetch Caleb, the hired man, from the stable and have the youth hitch up a team to the wagon. When he looked over at Tom again he saw the lawman holding his injured hand. "Jesus, son, you'd better have my missus look after that burn before it gets infected," he said.

The hand felt as if it were on fire, and the outline of the gun barrel seemed burned in the flesh of his palm. He held his wrist gently, blowing cool air down onto the wound. Already the charred flesh was starting to blister.

Tom got slowly to his feet and went into the kitchen. Mrs. McBain had gone out to the stable to find Caleb, and Margo was standing in the middle of the room. She seemed dazed and uncomprehending when Tom asked her to find lard for his hand. He had to repeat the request twice more before she understood. He winced and groaned loudly when the girl's gentle fingers smeared the grease over the wound.

"I'm sorry," she whispered, blushing at her own clumsiness. She held her head down while she worked, but Tom could see her face clearly. Damn! he thought, she would have been a beautiful woman without the ugly scar. Her features were delicate, almost patrician, with deep-set brown eyes over her finely-chiseled nose and full lips. He let his eyes slip down, taking in the exciting flesh of her slender neck and swelling bosom under the calico dress she wore. She was slim, but there was nothing boyish about her body. Under other circumstances Tom would have found himself very attracted to Margo—scar or no scar. Now, bone weary and with his hand throbbing with pain he felt only pity for the girl. He watched as she tenderly removed the lard, taking with it bits of powder residue and dirt.

"Can you stand the pain if I clean it with alcohol?" she asked, looking up at him for the first time. Her eyes were full of concern, as if she were sharing his pain. "I'm afraid it'll become infected if I don't get it cleaner than this."

The very thought of dousing his wound with alcohol sent shudders through his lean body, but he knew she was right. He had seen men lose limbs or even their lives from unattended wounds less serious than his own. "Go ahead," he told her through clenched teeth. "Just get it over with quickly."

Tom had almost no clear memory of what happened after the girl filled a tin basin with whiskey from the bar and plunged his hand into the liquid inferno. He vaguely remembered trying not to scream from the excruciating pain, of failing, of hearing his own gasp of anguish echoing around the kitchen. Then, someone was leading him out of the kitchen and into a small bedroom at the rear of the adobe and pulling off his clothing and putting him into bed. After that everything was a blank—a merciful blank.

* * *

He awoke with a start in the middle of the night. For a moment he had no recollection of where he was. It was only when he felt the throbbing pain in his bandaged left hand that it all came back to him. His body was drenched in sweat despite the coolness of the night. Suddenly he knew he wasn't alone in the room. Someone was sitting on a chair beside the bed.

"Who's there?" he croaked, trying to sit up.

"It's me . . . Margo," a soft voice answered. Tom felt the girl's gentle hands pushing him back down onto the pillow. "I heard you moaning and I came in to sit with you," she went on, her face close enough that he could smell her fresh breath and the exciting aroma of her womanhood. "Just lay back and rest."

"What time is it?" he asked as she let her fingers run lightly back and forth over his scarred forehead.

"I don't know . . . about three, I suppose," she replied. "How does your hand feel?"

It hurt like blazes, but Tom told her that it was feeling better. He was weak and vulnerable from the pain, yet the girl's presence was making him forget his disabled hand. He tried to remember how long it had been since he had had a woman. Several weeks, and the female had only been a whore in a bordello behind the Bird Cage Theatre in Tombstone.

"How did you get this scar?" Margo asked in a soft whisper.

Tom told her, wondering if his own disfigurement made the girl feel some sort of kinship with him. Not that their situations were in any way comparable: His had come as the consequence of a fight between two equals—Margo's cruel wound had been inflicted through no fault of her own, and she would suffer as no man would in similar circumstances. Indeed, the slash across his forehead gave him a certain charm. Her scar made her ugly and unwanted in the eyes of most men.

Unwanted? he thought. That was a joke in light of

the way he was responding to her now. He could feel his sex warming under the covers, almost hear the way his heart was beating faster now as she leaned closer and her soft breasts touched his arm. Damn! he told himself. Stop it! Stop thinking about her that way. *She's lonely and grateful for you helping the McBains—nothing more.* To take advantage of her would be a gross violation of everything he stood for.

And yet he knew instinctively that Margo was feeling the same stirring urges within her own body. She had been taken captive by the Indians as a young girl but she was a woman now, one who had been cruelly initiated into the mysteries of sex by savages, and one for whom any normal male-female relationship was now impossible because of her grotesque appearance. And there was no mistaking the way she was pressing her body against his as she tenderly stroked his forehead.

"You'd better get back to bed," he whispered, fighting his own urges. "I'll be all right now, honestly."

"Don't send me away, please," she begged, her voice hardly audible even in the stillness of the darkened room. "I *want* to stay. You don't know how it's been all these months . . . I've been so lonely and unhappy . . . wanting to be loved but knowing that men couldn't stand to look at me without . . . without . . ."

She left the sentence unfinished, and Tom remembered what Sergeant Callahan had said to the girl . . . "without puking!" Jesus! Tom thought. How in the name of Christ could anyone be so cruel and heartless?

Suddenly her fingers left his head and she was standing up. For a moment he thought she was going to leave. Then he heard the soft rustle of her dress coming off those young limbs and he gasped in surprise and pleasure when she pulled the covers away and got into bed beside him, letting her heated flesh touch his own. It was one of the most wonderful sensations he had ever experienced. Her breasts were soft and yet mature, her nipples already rising and taut. One long leg came up to rest on his and he felt the burning wetness of her sex against his thigh, sending shudders of desire through him. Her full lips were trailing along his cheek and neck, tentatively at first, then more urgently as her breathing became labored.

"I . . . want you," she pleaded, sending another shudder through his body when her fingers touched his penis, encircling the hardening organ, stroking it gently, making him groan involuntarily with lust. She was like a young, inexperienced girl, wanting him terribly but unsure of herself and his response. Her lips were now working their way down over his chest, her tongue circling his nipples while her hair grazed his aroused flesh. She stroked him into a raging hardness, fervently, insistently, at the same time moving the raw wetness of herself in increasing erotic circles on his hip and thigh, driving him half-crazy with the want of her.

"No, please, honey," he begged, resisting yet surrendering to her at the same time, hating himself for being so weak, telling himself that it was wrong.

Her face came up to still his lips with her own. Her tongue came out, snaking into his mouth, devouring his as she slid up onto him, her slender legs on each side of his body, her vagina poised just above his sex, her breasts slowly moving back and forth over the hardness of his chest. There was nothing coy about her now. She was a woman in need of a man and she intended to satisfy the raging desire that inflamed her young loins.

Slowly, teasingly, she let herself come down until her lust-slickened vaginal lips were throbbing against the shuddering shaft of his manhood, sliding up and down, sending jolts of obscene excitement surging through him. The more he fought the terrible need he felt, the more insistent became her demands. Then, almost automatically, she raised her hips again and hesitated for a second, long enough to reach between them and grasp his shaft again, holding it upright against her beckoning warmth. The sensation of her curly tendrils of pubic hair almost drove him mad.

"Now," she whispered urgently. "Now!"

God help me for doing this! Tom thought, suddenly jerking his hips upward, feeling his lust-swollen spear part the slickness of her vaginal lips and slide up into her waiting belly. He heard her moan softly, then felt a tightening around his sex as she drew him further up inside her. It was like nothing he had ever experienced in his life, as if the whole of his being were centered in the warm, wet grasp of her. Every nerve in his body cried out with pleasure when she let her young flesh come down to meet the demanding upward movement. Her nipples were hard and swollen and pressing against his own, her tongue came back down onto his face and her heated breath was inciting him.

"Oh God, I want it . . . I want it," she cried out, twisting and turning herself, hopelessly speared atop him, grinding her body wantonly as Tom began to thrust upward. His movements were slow and savoring at first, then faster and harder as she coaxed him on in her pleading voice. She was like a suddenly uncaged beast, wild and uncaring, driving herself up and down, screaming and moaning for more and more of the unbearable pleasure. Her lips were all over his face and neck, nipping and biting while she ground her luscious bottom around his steaming hardness. Tom was panting for breath, unable to stop the desperate rush to his own pleasure. He used his good hand to knead and massage the slickness of her buttocks, forcing himself upwards so that his mouth could close over first one, then the other, swollen nipple, drawing them in, sucking on the sweetness there, responding to the gasps of renewed pleasure that flew from her lust-contorted mouth.

Then, just when he thought he could stand no more of the insane sexual joy, Margo's body tensed for a moment, then exploded again. The woman went wild, jamming herself up and down without regard for anything but the jolts of orgasmic wonder that swept through her. Her sex was like a tight glove around his own hardened shaft, milking it, refusing to let go, forcing him to share in her unbelievable and wanton ecstasy.

When it was finally over, she let her perspiring body come down to rest against his, his penis still trapped in the throbbing womb of her femininity. They lay there like that a long time, neither of them moving, both lost in their own thoughts. Then, at some point, Margo began sliding away. Tom murmured a protest, but the girl reached up with one hand and stilled his words. He felt her breasts gliding down along his stomach and then over his limp penis, making the shaft stir to life again when it felt the pulsating nipples touch the slick flesh. He wondered what she was doing. Suddenly he knew. Her body came to rest far down on the bed and her mouth suddenly touched his manhood. Using one hand to hold the flaccid organ upright, her lips opened and she was licking and sucking the shaft into a throbbing hardness even more acute than before. Tom had been holding his breath and he heard himself gasp in stunned surprise now as she began to move her head up and down over his steaming loins, sucking him in and out of her mouth, bringing him more pleasure than he had ever felt in all his life.

Tom had known whores who did this to men, but it was his own first experience with fellatio. He had always thought the thing depraved and animalistic. Now, as the girl worshipped his maleness with her mouth and tongue, he wondered if there was anything more pleasurable in the whole world. And he knew that Margo enjoyed it as much as he did.

Chapter Two

When Tom finally awoke at daybreak the next morning, Margo was gone. He lay there for a moment wondering if it had all been an obscene dream. He knew it had been real when he found the strands of the girl's hair entwined in his fingers, a reminder of how he had clutched her head while she urgently made love to him in that unbelievable way.

He got up quickly, groaning as he fumbled with his clothing. His wounded hand felt better, with only a dull throbbing to replace the searing pain of the evening before. Thrusting on his boots, he made his way down the corridor and into the dining room of the adobe, surprised to find Amos Wicklund at one of the tables. His old friend looked dead-tired as he ate the plate of potatoes and eggs in front of him.

"Amos!" Tom cried out, coming toward his friend. "When did you get in?"

Amos was almost twenty years older than Tom, but he carried his age well. Tall and heavy-set, he had the easy grace that came from years in the saddle. His dark hair was turning grey now, and the handlebar mustache seemed to accent the added lines in his face, but Amos was still an imposing man. He looked up and smiled at Tom.

"About thirty minutes ago, *amigo*," he replied, standing up taking Tom's hand. "I figured you'd need the rest what with your ruckus last night, so Mrs. McBain hustled me some breakfast before I came in to wake you. How's your hand, old son?"

"Not so bad," Tom smiled wryly. "I made the mistake of grabbing that bastard's gun barrel. Jesus, those things sure get hot, don't they? I assume you heard what happened here last night, huh?"

Amos chuckled to himself as he sat down again. Tom took the seat opposite, pouring himself a cup of steaming black coffee from the enameled pot between them.

"Yeh, I heard, *amigo*. I wish I'd have been here to see that stupid soldier when he tangled with you. The army ain't going to like it, you messing with one of their sergeants, though, old son. But, don't worry, I'll square it for you. Mrs. McBain said the poor bastard was half-dead when you finished with him."

"The fucker deserved whatever he got," Tom protested. "He had no right to come in here threatening these folks. To hell with that, though, Amos. What in the name of God am I doing up here?"

The smile left his friend's face. Amos didn't respond for a moment, sipping his coffee and staring at Tom with sadness on his wrinkled face.

"Bad news, I'm afraid," he said at last. "I'm sorry I couldn't put it in the wire, but we figured it would be best just to get you up here pronto." He paused again, then went on. "It's your brother Billy, Tom. He's in jail up in Allison."

The mention of his brother surprised Tom. Billy was two years his senior, a wild, reckless man with a penchant for getting himself into trouble of one kind or another all his life. The two brothers had come west together from Ohio almost fifteen years before, after their parents died in an influenza epidemic. Both brothers had been full of piss and vinegar in those days, drinking and whoring and, like most other young drifters, taking whatever work came along. They had let life carry them along from one town to another without thought of anything but their next drink or next whore. Then, Tom Cavenaugh had gradually tired of the aimless life and took up a lawman's badge. Billy had been puzzled by his brother's rejection of their carefree life, but unwilling to change himself. Over the years they had seen one another a dozen or so times. There was no lack of news about Billy, however. Tom had been able to keep track of his brother through other lawmen or the twice-yearly letters Billy had sent. The last Tom had heard, his brother was working on a cattle ranch in the Texas Panhandle.

"You'd better tell me about it, Amos," Tom said slowly, suddenly filled with apprehension. Billy's current troubles couldn't be minor ones if Amos had brought him the length of Arizona to discuss them, Tom knew.

"He's in a right pack of trouble this time, Tom," Amos went on. "Billy's in jail up in Allison on a charge of raping and killing some young Mexican girl. It don't look good for him, and that's a fact, *amigo*. The thing happened two weeks ago. Judge Manners . . . he's the circuit judge for this district, is scheduled to be in Allison next week. They'll be holding the trial then."

Tom Cavenaugh said nothing for a few moments, stunned by his friend's words. There had to be some mistake, he thought, as a sick feeling stirred in the pit of his stomach. Billy was wild, a troublemaker certainly, perhaps even capable of killing someone. But not a defenseless woman! And he was no rapist. No, it couldn't be true.

"That's a goddamned lie, Amos!" he said at last, shaking his head violently. "Maybe Billy and I haven't been close these last few years, but my brother would never do them things to a woman . . . not even a Mexican whore! Jesus, Amos, you don't believe it, do you?"

Amos Wicklund wished there was some way he could spare his friend the pain. He wished that he didn't have to answer Tom's question. But it was necessary. Neither of them had ever been less than completely honest with one another, no matter how difficult the situation. And this was no time to start.

"I haven't heard Billy's side of the thing, Tom," he replied, sadly. "And I won't be sitting on the jury that tries him, so my opinion ain't worth a nickel schooner of beer. The important thing is that you get up to Allison to be with Billy. Aaron Mason has given me permission to go up with you, *amigo*."

"Tell me what you know," Tom demanded hoarsely.

"I don't know all the details," Amos said. "I was in Prescott when the message came in from the deputy sheriff in Allison, a man named Townsend. They asked if Judge Manners could come up, or if they should transfer Billy to Prescott for the trial. Well, Judge Manners was already on the circuit, so he added Allison to the schedule. Like I said, he'll be there next week for the trial."

"What about the girl he's supposed to have killed?" Tom interrupted impatiently.

"A sixteen-year-old named Maria Gomez," Amos replied. "And, according to the information we got, she wasn't no whore, Tom. She was a respectable girl who worked as a maid for the town banker. Apparently Billy and some others cowboys rode into Allison a few weeks ago on their way to California. They got to drinking and gambling and ran out of money. Billy's friends drifted on, but your brother stayed after he took a shine to this girl. He got him some piss-ass job at the livery stable and was trying to get the girl to marry him, if you can believe that. Well, the talk was that she was something of a prick-tease and was leading him on. The deputy sheriff figures Billy got drunk the night of the killing and decided he was going to *take* what she wouldn't give him. It looks like he just got carried away. At any rate, the girl's employer heard some screams coming from the little shack where the girl slept and went out to see what the ruckus was. He found the girl dead and Billy in bed with the body . . . him naked as a jaybird and with scratches and blood all over him. Like I said, Tom, it don't look good for Billy."

"You're sure it's Billy?" Tom asked, grasping at straws. "I mean, shit, there could be another Billy Cavanaugh in this damned country, couldn't there?"

"There's no mistake, old son," Amos said, shaking his head. "According to the deputy sheriff in Allison, Billy had been bragging about having a U. S. Marshal for a brother. They thought he was just shooting the shit to impress folks. No, *amigo*, it's Billy, all right. Look, let me change clothes and then we'll ride out. We can be in Allison by tomorrow night if we hustle. That'll give us five or six days before Judge Manners gets there."

Shaking his head, Tom Cavenaugh pushed himself away from the table, wincing when he bumped his bandaged hand on his chair.

"I'm thankful for your offer, Amos," he said firmly. "But, this is family business. I'll go up alone." He hesitated, waving aside his friend's protest as he unpinned the marshal's star from his vest and put it on the table in front of Amos. "Billy is my kin, not yours, and I don't want any of this rubbing off on you."

"What in the hell is *this* for?" Amos said, surprised, looking at the lawman's star.

"I've never used my badge to help Billy before, Amos, and I don't intend to start now. If he's guilty of this crime, which I don't believe for a goddamned minute, then he'll hang and to hell with him. If he's innocent, well, I don't need a star to prove it. Keep it for me, Amos. I'll ask for it back if Billy goes free."

"And if he doesn't?"

"Then I won't have any further use for it," Tom said bitterly.

Amos shook his head again. He knew better than to

try and argue the point with his friend. Tom Cavenaugh could be more stubborn than a mule when his mind was set, and there was nothing Amos could say or do to make his friend see reason.

"You'd be making a serious mistake, old son," he said softly, putting the star in his pocket. "Billy may be blood kin, but we all ride our own trail and nobody's going to think less of you for anything he's done."

It was plain talk, the kind Amos Wicklund would have gotten from Tom Cavenaugh had the situation been reversed. But the words were wasted.

"At least let me go with you, Tom," Amos added earnestly.

"Don't press it," Tom replied, wanting his friend to understand but, at the same time, in no mood to argue. "I know you mean well, *amigo*," he went on, his voice softening. "But, please, I have to do this my own way. I'd be thankful if you wished me luck, though."

"*Mucho fortuna*, for what it's worth," Amos said, nodding. "You're a damned fool, *amigo*, and that's a fact. I'll be riding back to Prescott after I rest up a bit. If you need me, get word to me there and I'll come up as quick as I can."

"Thanks, Amos," Tom told his friend.

He left the dining room after retrieving his saddlebags and gun, then went across the yard to the stable. McBain seemed surprised to see him. He told Tom that Sergeant Callahan had been sent to Prescott with the hired hand. When Tom tried to pay the station master for his food, night's lodging, and the stabling of his horse, McBain shook his head, refusing to accept any payment.

"It's on the house, son," he told Tom. McBain was filled with curiosity that Tom was leaving so quickly, but he assumed that it had something to do with Sergeant Callahan. Well, it was none of his business, he told himself, going into the stable to get Tom's horse.

While McBain was saddling Double Eagle, Tom heard Margo call out his name. Turning toward the adobe, he saw the girl coming toward him.

"You're leaving?" she asked, obviously distressed.

"I'm sorry, Margo," he said quietly, at a loss for words. "I've got business up in Allison . . . business that can't wait."

She blushed deeply, turning away.

"You think I'm a whore, don't you!" she said bitterly, tears forming in her eyes. "You don't have to say it . . . I know what you're thinking. You're afraid if you stay I might get ideas. That's it, isn't it?" She thrust her hands up to cover her scarred face. "Don't look at me that way, damn you! I know how ugly I am! I just thought that . . . that . . ."

She burst into tears and ran back toward the house before Tom could stop her. He watched, torn between his desire to go after her and tell the distraught women that her disfigurement made no difference to him, and his burning need to be on his way to Allison. Billy's life might be hanging in the balance, he told himself, deciding that Margo's obvious pain was less important than his brother's life. It was one of the most difficult decisions Tom had ever been called upon to make, but he had no real choice. After it was over he could explain things to Margo, make her see that she *was* important to him. For now there was only the uncertainty of Billy's fate.

When McBain brought his saddled horse out to him, Tom pulled himself up into the saddle and rode off without looking back.

Tom rode hard all morning. His horse was well-rested, much more so than the troubled lawman. As he rode, Tom tried to make sense out of what Amos Wicklund had told him. His mind kept coming back to the same argument— *Billy couldn't rape and then kill some defenseless young girl!* Men change over the years,

Tom knew, and every merciless killer he had ever known had once been an innocent youth. Still, for all the troubles Billy had managed to get himself into, none had involved violence upon any female. He prayed that some mistake had been made, that Billy could provide some explanation for the terrible charges of which he now stood accused.

Tom's horse threw a shoe early that afternoon.

"God damn the luck!" Tom muttered aloud, cursing himself, the hapless animal, and all the fates which had made him choose the old Indian trail through the Mogollon Mountains, instead of staying on the main stagecoach route. He had hoped to save a few hours. Now he was stranded with a disabled mount and there was little likelihood of him meeting anyone for at least another ten miles when he would rejoin the main trail at the small settlement of Pine Mesa. There was nothing to do except walk out, then get a fresh mount there. It would be tough going for the horse, and it would slow him down, but he knew he couldn't abandon the animal, no matter how desperate was his own need to travel fast.

Forcing himself to move slowly, he started off. The mountain trail was worn as smooth as a highway by the centuries of Yavapai Indian travel, and he could still make out the rubble of old campsites along the way. The air was crisp and clear and thin at this altitude, a welcome relief from the oppressive heat of the desert below.

He forced himself to stop after an hour's travel, watering the limping animal from his canteen and permitting himself the luxury of a smoke before going on. He was hungry, but there was no thought of food. That would have to wait. His hand was filled with pain again, the result of his palm slapping against his stomach as he had ridden. He was tempted to change the dressing. Deciding against it, he stood up and knocked the ashes from his pipe, then ground them into the dust with his boot heel. About eight miles to go, he guessed, inspecting his horse's bruised hoof before setting off again.

Suddenly he froze as he heard the sound of horses moving up the trail in the direction he was going. He estimated them to be a quarter mile or so off, and at least six in the group. He knew from the sound of metal on rock that they were not Indian ponies. The sounds were as welcome as any he had ever heard.

Tom waited, positioning himself in the middle of the trail so that he could be clearly seen when the riders rounded the bend a hundred or so yards off in the distance. It seemed likely that they were trappers or prospectors, for this trail was rarely used by anyone but Indians.

A few minutes later he could make out voices speaking in English. Then, two riders appeared, followed by a small group of horses being herded by a third man. The men had not seen Tom yet and he had time to size them up. They were dressed in trail garb, with sugarloaf sombreros tilted back on their heads, and one of the men in front had a carbine resting lightly across his saddle horn. He could see that the front two were thirtyish, with long hair and weatherbeaten features.

Suddenly one of the men saw him. They reined in, looked him over for a moment, and then the one with the carbine rode slowly forward, watching Tom with wary eyes.

"Howdy," he said when he was about ten feet away. His thumb was resting lightly on the carbine's hammer, ready for trouble. "What you doing out here, mister?"

The man's voice was neither friendly nor hostile, simply matter-of-factly curious.

Tom quickly explained his situation, staring past the rider to the half-dozen horses the men were herding. Even at this distance he could see they were excellent animals, strong and healthy. "Look," he went on. "I'm in a tight spot with my horse like he is and me needing to get to Allison quickly. Would you be of a mind to sell me one of those horses? I'd pay top dollar."

"Can't do it, mister," the rider answered, shaking his head. "Those are army mounts me and the boys are running over to Fort Whipple. The quartermaster there has already bought and paid for 'em. Sorry, but we can't help you."

"Then, damn it, *loan* me one," Tom asked, impatiently. "I'll see that the army gets it back. I'll give you a receipt and turn the horse in to the nearest military post as quick as I can rustle up a new mount."

He reached into the back pocket of his jeans to bring out his wallet to show the rider he had money and identification. His warrant as a U. S. marshal was still in the oilskin, a fact he suddenly remembered. Thank Christ he hadn't given *that* to Amos Wicklund along with his star, he told himself. His arm stopped in midair as he heard the ominous click of the carbine's hammer being pulled.

"Just hold it, mister," the rider warned. "Bring that arm back where I can see it. That's right, nice and easy. Now, unbuckle your belt and let it drop so we don't have any misunderstandings."

"Damn it, I'm a U. S. marshal," Tom protested angrily. Technically he was not, his service temporarily ending when he turned in his star to Amos. But the lie seemed harmless enough in view of his need for a horse. He did as he was ordered, however, unbuckling his gunbelt and letting it slip down around his legs and come to rest on the trail. He watched with mounting impatience as the rider lifted his left hand and signaled for the other two men to ride forward.

"How come you didn't say you were a marshal right off?" the man asked while he waited for his companions. "And, I don't see no star on your vest, mister."

"My identification is in my pocket," Tom replied, trying to hold his rising temper. "Look, you've no call to draw on me like that. Let me prove who I am and take one of those horses. As a federal officer I've got the right to confiscate government property in an emergency."

"What kind of emergency is this? How come you're in such an all-fired hurry to get to Allison?"

Tom was in a bad situation and he knew it. Without one of the horses he wouldn't reach Allison before morning, even assuming he could pick up another horse in Pine Mesa. His need for the animal outweighed his normal reticence and he decided to tell the rider the truth.

"I am a marshal," he said earnestly, "and my identification is in my back pocket. It's really none of your business, mister, but I've got a brother in jail in Allison and I've got to get up there as quick as I can. Like I said, it's none of your business, but I'll put all my cards on the table for one of those horses."

The two other riders had reached them now. One watched the horses while the other looked at Tom, then over at his partner.

"What's up, Lacey?" he asked.

The man named Lacey ignored the question, staring at Tom.

"Let's see that identification, mister," he ordered.

Tom pulled out the oilskin pouch and extracted his warrant card, handing it up to the rider. The man scanned it slowly, then handed it to the other man. The second cowboy blushed, giving it back.

"Hell, Lacey, you know I can't read much," he said. "What's this all about."

"This fella is U. S. Marshal Tom Cavenaugh," Lacey replied slowly. "He's on his way to Allison 'cause his brother is in jail there. His horse throwed a shoe and he wants one of our horses."

"Cavenaugh?" the second man asked, his eyes widening. "Ain't that the name of the . . ."

Lacey stopped his friend before he could finish the

sentence. Then, easing himself off his horse, he tripped the hammer of his carbine and thrust it into its saddle scabbard. The expression on his face had softened when he addressed Tom again.

"You can have the horse, mister," he said quietly. "But, you're too late to see your brother."

"What in the hell does that mean?" Tom demanded.

"I'm sorry, mister, but there was a lynching in Allison last night. The townsmen strung up some cowboy drifter named Billy Cavenaugh."

Tom's face went white and it was all he could do to keep from screaming out in impotent rage and frustration. *Oh God*, he thought bitterly, *I'm too late! The sonsabitches have killed Billy*!

Lacey and his companion looked on, shaking their heads as Tom tried to control himself. His stomach was churning, his hands trembling helplessly. His mind raced with horrible thoughts of his brother being slaughtered by a bloodthirsty mob who couldn't wait to give him a fair trial.

"What happened?" he asked at last, forcing himself to speak.

"Well, me and the boys here were in Allison last night to pick up these horses for the army. We come in the day before and we heard about your brother killing this greaser girl a couple of weeks ago. Folks was pretty riled up about the murder, I guess. About six o'clock last night we was having a drink in the saloon when a couple of men started saying it wasn't right for your brother to have no trial . . . that he'd raped this girl and then killed her, and he should be strung up right then and there. I swear to God, mister, me and the boys didn't have no part of that talk. Hell, we didn't know the girl or your brother. They kind of argued back and forth for a while, with some of them saying he should have a trial, but most of them saying the girl didn't get no trial . . . so why should he? Besides, they said, they'd give him a judge . . . good old *Judge Lynch*!"

"Lacey's right, mister," the second man interrupted. "Those that wanted to lynch your brother had the rest of them all whipped up before anyone could stop them."

"Who was doing the talking?" Tom asked in a strangled voice.

"Some asshole named Gilman or Hilman, or something like that," Lacey answered. "He kept at everybody . . . buying 'em drinks and saying they weren't real men if they didn't string up this fella. Hell, you know how that goes, mister . . . get the mob liquored up and show 'em a rope and they'd lynch *anybody*! This Gilman or Hilman, or whatever, he finally said fuck it, he weren't no coward, that he'd do the job himself."

"Go on."

"Well, the whole damned saloon emptied out real quick. The funny thing is, by the time they got to the jail, half the men in town were already there. Me and the boys kind of tagged along but, like I told you, we couldn't stop them, and we damned sure didn't have any part in it. They broke down the jail door and dragged the poor bastard . . . I'm sorry, mister, I mean they dragged your *brother* out into the street. He was screaming and begging for mercy, but they didn't pay him no mind. A couple of greasers tried to kill him right on the spot, jumping around and flashing their knives and yelling for blood."

"Where in fuck was the sheriff?"

"We didn't see hide nor hair of any lawman," Lacey went on. Anyhow, they dragged your brother behind the livery stable and used the big old oak tree there to string him up. By that time the preacher come running and tried to stop them, but it was too late, and that's a fact."

Tom turned and walked away, too overcome with emotion to want to hear anymore. He stood there for a few minutes, tears of grief welling up in his eyes and spilling down over his cheeks. Lacey whispered to his companion to pick out the best horse in the bunch and transfer the saddle from Tom's animal to the new mount. While that was being done, he walked over to where Tom stood and put his hand on the lawman's shoulder. Tom swung around, fire in his eyes.

"Was there anybody in that whole goddamned town beside the preacher who tried to stop the lynching?" he growled. "Even one?"

"If there was, we didn't see him," Lacey replied, shaking his head. "Look, Marshal Cavenaugh, we've cut out the best horse for you. Me and the boys are going to rest and have some beans and coffee. You're welcome to share it."

"No, I'll be on my way," Tom replied, talking a pencil stub and a worn notebook from his shirt pocket and writing out a receipt for the horse. He handed it to Lacey. "This Gilman or Hilman . . . the man who was doing all the agitating. Can you tell me anything more about him?"

"Well, he's about your age, give or take a year or two, a little over six feet, I'd guess, and mean looking. He was with a bunch of wranglers from one of the local ranches. If I had to guess I'd say he was one of them, but I ain't for sure. That's all I know, mister. What about your horse? You want us to take him with us to Fort Whipple?"

Tom thought for a moment, then nodded absently. "I'd be obliged if you did," he said. "Ask the quartermaster there to keep him for a couple of weeks. I'll pick him up and swap animals on my way back through."

The saddled horse was waiting and Tom strode over and mounted the animal, taking the reins from the cowboy. He touched his fingers to the brim of his Stetson in salute, dug his spurs into the horse's flanks, and rode off without a word. In a few moments the horse and rider had disappeared around the bend in the trail.

"Jesus, that's a hard way for a man to find out his brother's been kilt," the second cowboy said to Lacey. "I sure as hell feel sorry for the poor bastard, no matter what his brother did to that greaser girl."

"Save your sympathy for the fuckers who strung up the brother," Lacey replied laconically. "The marshal is a hard case, and that's a fact. He ain't going to let the thing rest, Jim, and that's *another* fact."

Amy Cartwright was more unhappy than at any time since she had married Harold Cartwright and allowed the banker to bring her to Arizona from her home in Chicago almost two years before. At twenty-one, she was almost fifteen years younger than her husband, a tall, beautiful woman with delicate—almost patrician—features surrounded by masses of golden hair that swirled in honey-hued curls around her lovely shoulders. Unusually tall for a woman, her body was perfectly proportioned, from her slender legs up to the magnificently swelling breasts that strained against the soft silk of her dresses.

It was strange and unsettling, this unhappiness. She had everything most women could want—a handsome husband with money and power, one who would be governor of Arizona someday, or even its United States Senator when the territory became a state. Their large frame home on the outskirts of Allison was a mansion, really, not like those back east, of course, but large and beautiful and imposing for this part of the country. As Harold Cartwright's wife she was the undisputed social leader of the community, a woman to be deferred to. And, along with her undeniable beauty there was intelligence and wit, as well.

And yet she wished desperately that she had never married Harold Cartwright, never left the excitement and glamor of Chicago for this dreary little frontier town, filled with small-minded people who shared none of her cultural or intellectual interests. She was the social leader all right, she thought bitterly, but of what? A pack of vulgar men and women of no taste or refinement. There were none with whom she could even carry on a conversation about art or literature or music. Adding to her depression was her husband's increasing and irrational jealousy. He tortured them both with his dark thoughts whenever she even smiled at another man, however innocently, certain that her sexual inhibitions with him were only a ploy to disguise her unbridled passion in some other man's arms.

Sex had been, for the virginal young bride, a rude and painful initiation into adulthood. She had wanted and expected romance and tenderness from her husband. She got, instead, physical pain and thoughtlessness from Harold. He took her with no thought for her pleasure, only his own. As a result, she quickly came to see sex as something to be endured but not enjoyed. When she allowed him to make love to her the act was devoid of warmth or joy. She lay beneath him, her face turned away and contorted with disgust at his animal-like grunts and his sweaty body. And the more she resisted him, the more angry and jealous he became, until their marriage was hardly more than an armed truce.

Things had become even more frustrating when Harold insisted on hiring Maria Gomez as a maid several months before. Amy had been opposed to the move, arguing that the saucy young Mexican girl was too irresponsible and untrustworthy to bring into their home. Harold had been adamant, pointing out that they *needed* a servant and that it would take weeks to bring one out from back east. Amy wasn't stupid. She quickly discovered that Harold had more in mind for Maria Gomez than just household chores. She saw the way he looked lustfully at the girl's nubile young body, the way Maria responded shamelessly by teasing the banker with her olive flesh and outrageous impudence to every man who visited the house.

Yet, Amy was almost certain that her husband wasn't sleeping with the girl. At least not yet. Many of the townsmen had Mexican sluts for mistresses, of course, and one had only to see some of the children in that part of Allison set aside as the Mexican ghetto to recognize that they had white blood in them. She knew that Harold would find some way to seduce the girl and then rub her nose in the obscenity of it all. And everyone in Allison would know that the banker was sleeping with his sluttish maid and laugh at her, Amy thought in desperation.

Still, it had been a terrible blow to Amy when the girl was raped and then strangled by the drunken cowboy drifter, Billy Cavenaugh. Mercifully, Amy had been away in Prescott on a shopping trip the night it happened. She had returned two days later to find Maria's mutilated body already buried, the girl's killer in jail awaiting trial.

Then, almost as shocking, the men of Allison had erupted in an orgy of rage the evening before and dragged Maria's killer from his jail cell and lynched him. The news had reached them as Deputy Sheriff Miles Townsend and Harold were drinking brandy and having an after-dinner cigar in the billard room. She could still close her eyes and see the stunned expression on Sheriff Townsend's face and, more disturbing, the smug, half-smile that flickered across her husband's lips at the terrible news.

She was still reeling from the ugly incidents the next afternoon when she served her husband lunch. Incredibly, the death of Billy Cavenaugh had seemed to lift Harold's spirits, to wash away the anxiety and irritability he had felt since Maria's murder. He smiled and made little jokes with his wife while he ate—as if nothing had happened.

"Maybe you and I should take that little trip up to Denver I've been promising you, honey," Cartwright suggested teasingly. "Maybe even all the way to San Francisco. Do us both good to get away for a while."

"I'd like nothing better than to get away from this awful place," Amy replied vehemently. "But for good . . . not just on a vacation!"

Surprised, Harold stayed his fork in midair, staring at his wife. "Damn it, Amy, there you go complaining again," he protested. "This is our home and that's all there is to it. What is it, are you still upset about that thing last night?"

"Two people are murdered and you act as though it's just an everyday thing," she answered sarcastically. "I hate it! I hate this town and everyone in it! You don't know how sorry I am I ever let you talk me into leaving Chicago!"

"*Two* people murdered?" he asked, ignoring the rest of his wife's outburst. "Oh, I see what you mean. Hell, honey, they didn't murder that bastard Cavenaugh . . . they just strung him up and saved the expense of a trial. Now, I don't hold with lynching a man, usually, but he deserved it, didnt' he? The things he did to poor little Maria before he killed her would make a man puke. You weren't here, so you didn't see her body after he finished with her . . ."

"Stop it!" she cried out, putting her hands over her ears in protest, trying to shut out the awful words. "I don't want to hear!"

Harold smiled shyly, enjoying baiting his wife. God-damned cold fish! he accused silently. She had put him through hell by withholding her lush, beautiful body from him—never giving an inch, making him feel like some sort of animal for wanting what any normal man wants from a woman? Well, by Christ, he thought, she's not getting away from me. She's not running back to Chicago so she can take up with one of her lovers!

"What's the matter?" he laughed mirthlessly. "You never liked Maria anyway, so why should it bother you to hear how that lowdown drifter tore up her insides before he went crazy and killed her. Did I tell you that Doctor Mayberry said the bastard had even forced her to use her *mouth* on him? Imagine that, Amy!"

"Stop it!" she screamed. "Why are you torturing me like this, Harold?"

"I'm not doing the torturing around here, darling," he growled. "It's you who's making my life hell! How do you think I feel when my own wife won't let me make love to her? You haven't let me touch you since that thing happened to Maria." His voice suddenly softened as he thought of Amy's beautiful soft body. "Don't look at me like that, Amy. I'm not some sort of monster . . . I'm a man and men need sex and pleasure from a woman. If you'd just relax you could learn to like it, too."

She turned and fled from the dining room before he could say any more. Shocked, he watched her retreating back and then listened to her footsteps on the stairway and the slamming of her bedroom door. Suddenly he was angry, more angry than he had been in weeks.

"Damned women!" he cursed, pushing away his food and standing up. "They're all alike . . . every damned one of them . . . shaking their asses around and driving a man half-crazy, then freezing up on him."

He stripped off his jacket and threw it on the chair. *By Jesus, I'm sick of this*, he thought. *She's my wife and she's going to start acting like a wife should*!

It was almost time for him to go back and open up the bank for the afternoon, but Harold Cartwright decided to let his clerk take care of that. He went toward the stairway, ripping off his tie and unbuttoning his shirt. His genitals were beginning to throb painfully as he went upstairs, his mind filled with erotic thoughts of his wife's naked body. He wanted her very badly. And he was going to have her!

Amy looked up in surprise when she saw her husband throw open the bedroom door and storm inside.

"What do you want?" she gasped, pulling the silk coverlet up over her body.

"What do you *think* I want?" he scowled. He let his eyes roam over the exciting contours of her reclining body, pausing briefly at the swelling of her breasts, then slowly down along her stomach to the soft indentation where her thighs came together so beautifully.

"Please, Harold, you're frightening me," she pleaded, moving away when he sat down at the side of the bed and reached for her. "No! I don't want you to touch me! I don't feel well!"

"Oh?" he sneered. "You were feeling all right last night when you were making eyes at Sheriff Townsend behind my back. You didn't think I noticed, did you? Is he one of your lovers, too?"

Amy could hardly believe her ears. Of all the men she knew, Miles Townsend was the last person she would have wanted as a lover. How could her husband degrade and humiliate her like this? She wondered. Didn't he understand how irrational his baseless accusations were?

But Harold had gone too far to back down now. His mind was filled with dark, ugly thoughts. "You aren't fooling me," he went on, cruelly. "No normal woman could be as cold as you claim to be. I work my ass off to give you all this luxury and you're playing around on me. Admit it, damn it!"

She watched in horror while he stood up and tore at his clothing, stripping himself naked. Cringing, her face flushed, too stunned to speak, she moaned and tried to pull away when he grabbed the coverlet and jerked it away from her body, then climbed into the bed beside her. The evidence of his arousal was pressing against her hip, almost making her ill.

"No, please, don't," she pleaded as he ripped at her clothing. "There's no other man, I swear it!"

Her dress and underclothing were in shreds and he brutally pulled her thighs apart, exposing her genitals, thrusting his hand down into the quivering flesh there, her resistance only inflaming him more.

"Stop that fidgeting and lay still," he ordered, holding her thighs apart while he rolled atop her. "I'm getting what's mine, damn it!"

Frightened half out of her wits, Amy knew there was no point in fighting him. He was beyond reason, irrational with his obscene lust. Her only salvation was to let him have his way with her, to get it over quickly or drown in her own shame and humiliation. Hating both her husband and herself, she let her legs go limp, shuddering with disgust when she felt the heat of his manhood brutally sliding into her stomach.

"That's better," he moaned, reaching up under her buttocks and pulling her more tightly against his hairy loins, then driving himself downward with a furious, soul-wrenching thrust that left her gasping with pain.

Every jarring movement in and out of her body was like torture. He was slobbering now, his spittle dripping down onto her breasts and throat, and he tried to kiss her, growling like an animal when she turned her head away.

On and on the salacious act went until she was ready to scream for mercy. Her mind was in a raging turmoil of hatred and self-pity until, mercifully, with a low, gutteral cry of pleasure, he began spewing out his heated juices.

When his movements stopped a few minutes later he collapsed atop her, driving the breath from her trembling flesh. He lay there, not moving, a smug smile on his sweaty face. "This is the way it's going to be from now on," he warned. "No more arguments . . . no more excuses. You're going to act like a wife, understand?"

"I hate you!" she shouted up at him, unable to control her rage, sobbing wildly, pushing him away. "You're no better than the man they hanged last night!

No, you're even worse! At least he put *his* victim out of her misery when it was over!"

She leaped up from the bed and ran out of the room, sobbing loudly. Cartwright watched her go, knowing that things would be tense between them for a few days, that she would be sullen and angry, like always. But, he didn't care. He had finally mastered his beautiful young wife. All his previous pleading and cajoling had produced no results, he had always come away from her bed depressed and unsatisfied. Now, by using force on the headstrong young woman he had made her accept her lawful role as his wife. Maybe that's what all women need, he mused as he climbed out of bed and used the chamberpot to relieve himself. Give them a taste of violence, break their spirits like you would an untamed horse. Then they could be ridden safely and at will. Well, if that was what Amy wanted, the banker was more than prepared to give her trouble in spades!

Everything seemed to be falling into place, he thought smugly. The problem of Maria's death had resolved itself now that Billy Cavenaugh was dead. The episode was closed, and he could get on with his other business, direct his full energy to seeing that the railroad would come through Allison and insure his increased wealth and power.

It pleased Harold Cartwright how he had so efficiently handled the matter of the cowboy drifter. Even so, Cartwright had had a few bad moments yesterday when he learned that Cavenaugh's brother—a U. S. marshal—was on his way to Allison. But he had taken care of things like he always did. Let the brother come ahead, he thought; let him bring all the lawmen in the territory! The matter was closed now. Judge "Lynch" had seen to that.

The banker dressed again and went downstairs, untroubled and ready to face the afternoon. For a moment he was tempted to go back upstairs and make love to his wife again just to insure that she clearly understood her new position. He changed his mind, remembering that Jim Conroy was coming in that afternoon to talk over the new loan he wanted. This was no time to offend Conroy by keeping him waiting, he told himself, not after what the rancher had done for him.

Harold Cartwright was a happy man as he went out into the sunshine and hitched his buggy for the short ride into town.

Chapter Three

Deputy Sheriff Miles Townsend was a deeply disturbed man as he sat in his small office at the front of the Allison jail and labored over his report on the lynching of Billy Cavenaugh. The report would go to Sheriff Jack Buchanan, Townsend's superior, the chief law enforcement officer of Yavapai County. And Miles knew that Buchanan wouldn't like what he read.

Both Miles Townsend and Jack Buchanan believed in the premise that every accused man—no matter how despicable the crime—had a right to his day in court. It had been different in the past, of course, when every man was his own judge, jury, and hangman. There were few lawmen and even fewer courts, and a man had the right to take the law into his own hands to protect himself and his property. But now, with homesteaders and ranchers and miners swarming into the territory, it was supposed to be different. There were duly appointed courts to take care of people like Billy Cavenaugh. Just a few days more would have seen the arrival of Judge Manners from Prescott, and an almost certain verdict of guilty, followed by a legal hanging that no one could question.

Instead, a drunken mob urged on by a few hotheads had circumvented justice and made a mockery of the law in their thirst for vengeance. In the process, those who had lynched Billy Cavenaugh had demonstrated how thin the veneer of society still was in places like Arizona.

But it wasn't only the fact of Billy Cavenaugh's death that bothered Miles. That was bad enough, of course, but Billy would have died in any event. Far worse was his nagging feelings of guilt over having left the jail unguarded so that he could dine with Harold Cartwright and his wife. The invitation had been entirely unexpected, the first he had ever received from the banker, and he had let his vanity get the better of his judgment. In all his years as a lawman, Miles Townsend had never lost a prisoner to a lynch mob. He blamed himself now, knowing he should have refused Cartwright's invitation. His responsibility had been clear: A prisoner in custody came before any social consideration. But, Miles had failed in his primary duty, and Billy Cavenaugh had died.

Even worse yet, the wire from Prescott the day before had confirmed that Billy was, indeed, the brother of a U. S. marshal, and that Marshal Tom Cavenaugh would be in Allison in the near future. Like everyone else, Townsend had discounted Billy's boast as just another of the accused man's fanciful lies. Now he would have to tell a brother peace officer that Billy had been dragged out of the jail and murdered by a mob.

He finished the report and blotted it, then slipped the pages into an envelope, addressed it to Sheriff Buchanan, and put it aside.

Sighing deeply, he took another sheet of foolscap and started to write out his own resignation. He suspected the sheriff would tear it up, but Miles felt he had no other choice but to make the gesture. In any event, his effectiveness in Allison was at an end. The townspeople were sullen and refused to give him any information on who had started the lynch talk. That hurt. Miles had known most of them as good friends. Now they were like strangers, as if the guilt and shame were his rather than their own.

He had just finished the resignation when the jail door burst open. Miles looked up to find himself staring into the coldest eyes he had ever confronted. There was no doubt in his mind who his angry visitor was, even though he saw no star on the other man's vest.

"You'll be Billy's brother, I suppose?" he asked quietly, not getting up.

"I am, damn your soul!" Tom Cavenaugh snarled. "And you'll be the cowardly bastard who let a mob lynch your prisoner!"

Forcing himself to keep calm, Miles Townsend stood up. "Do you want the truth of it, mister? Or are you just looking to have your pound of flesh without knowing what really happened here last night?"

"I already *know* what happened!" Tom went on, his rage building. "A mob broke in here and hanged my brother without a trial. And, instead of protecting your prisoner, like it's your sworn duty to do, you weren't anywhere around. Where were you, Townsend? Drunk in one of the saloons? Or hiding under a bed somewhere like the cowardly sonofabitch you are!"

Townsend could see that Tom Cavenaugh was dangerously close to drawing down on him. In a way he couldn't blame the other man. His own emotions would be the same in the situation were reversed. Still, he wanted no part of any more killing.

"It wasn't that way, mister," he replied. "But, to tell you the straight of it, I had a hard time looking at myself in the mirror this morning. I made a serious mistake last night and I'll take the blame for that if it's any comfort to you. But, by God, the next time you call me a coward you'd best be ready to draw."

The warning seemed to have the desired effect. Tom Cavenaugh continued to stare angrily at Miles Townsend for a few more moments. Then, slowly, his body relaxed and his expression softened.

"Tell me what happened," he whispered.

Townsend needed a drink badly, as did Tom Cavenaugh. He took a bottle of cheap rye whiskey and two tumblers from his desk drawer, pouring them each a glassful. Tom took the glass gratefully, downing the whiskey in one long draught. When he was finished, Townsend poured him another, motioning for Tom to sit down.

"How much do you know about this business of Billy and the girl?" Townsend asked after they were both seated.

"Just what Amos Wicklund told me," Tom replied. "Billy and I came west together from Ohio years ago, but we went our separate ways a long time since. The last I heard, Billy was punching cows on a ranch over in Texas."

"I might as well begin at the beginning then," Miles said, settling himself in his chair and leaving the whiskey bottle between them. The deputy sheriff was not a particularly sympathetic man by nature, but he tried to present Billy Cavenaugh's character fairly as he told Tom how his brother had ridden into Allison with his two friends several weeks before. The three cowboy drifters had been on their way to California, they told everyone, after wintering on a cattle ranch in the Texas Panhandle. Their intention had been only to spend a night or two drinking and gambling and whoring in Allison's pleasure palaces. Unfortunately, the money they had saved was soon gone. "Those boys didn't give me any trouble and I didn't give them any," Miles said. "But, I don't like drifters in my town and, to tell the truth, I wasn't unhappy when Billy's friends moved on. And I wasn't overjoyed that Billy stayed on, either. I knew there was going to be trouble."

"Why?"

"Billy had taken a shine to Maria Gomez, and that was bad news as far as I could see. Maria was only fifteen years old . . . almost twenty years younger than your brother. Oh, I know how fast these greaser girls age, but she was a damned prick-tease to boot!

She worked for Mr. and Mrs. Cartwright . . . he's the local banker. They kept a pretty tight rein on her, but Maria was always making up to some man or other. Hell, every time she'd come into town all the young bucks trailed after Maria like a pack of dogs after a bitch in heat. I swear, she was a sexy little thing, all right, flouncing around in them tight skirts and blouses that showed off her tits! She could drive any man half-crazy, that girl."

"What about her and Billy?" Tom asked impatiently.

"I'm coming to that," Miles said. "Like I told you, Billy took a shine to the girl. When his friends left Allison, he took a job over at the livery stable and feed store so he could stay around and moon over her. He even bragged around town that he was going to marry Maria and take her to California with him. Nobody believed him, of course. We all figured your brother would up and skedaddle as soon as he managed to screw her. To tell the truth, Billy was making a right fool of himself over that girl. Shit, everybody in town was laughing at him."

"What about the girl? Was she leading him on?"

"Hell yes! Every time she came to town on an errand or had a day off, she and Billy was together. She seemed to like treating him like a dog in front of other people, jabbering away at him in Spanish and telling him what a fool he was. Billy didn't seem to care, though. He just took it all and came back for more."

"You don't think he was sleeping with her, then?"

Townsend shrugged.

"No, I don't think so. Maria was the kind of girl who'd lead a man on, but wouldn't let him touch the merchandise, if you know what I mean. It was just a game with her. I tried to talk to Billy and tell him which way was up, but he wouldn't listen to me. Finally, after the banker caught Billy sneaking out to see Maria one night and ran him off, I sat Billy down and tried to talk turkey to him, told him he'd end up in jail if he didn't leave the girl alone. Billy just laughed and told me to mind my own business. A week later Maria was dead."

"Go on."

"There ain't too much more to tell. On Monday of last week Harold Cartwright rode into town about two o'clock in the morning and woke me up. Mrs. Cartwright had gone to Prescott the day before to do some shopping, and Cartwright had invited a couple of the local businessmen out to play some poker . . . Jeb Fallon and Marcus Owens. About eight o'clock, Maria had finished up her chores and went out to the shack in the back of the house where she slept. Well, sir, about one-thirty Cartwright and his friends heard some screaming from out back. Cartwright got his shotgun and they all went out to see what the ruckus was about. They figured Billy had snuck out to see the girl again. It was Billy all right. He was dead drunk and passed out on the bed. Maria Gomez was . . ."

He paused before going on.

"You want to hear this, son? It ain't very pretty."

"Tell me," Tom insisted.

"Well, like I said, Billy was passed out on Maria's bed . . . naked as a jaybird and with scratches all over him. Maria was naked, too, and she was almost dead. She'd been used pretty badly. Billy had tied her arms and feet to the bedposts and then gagged her so she couldn't scream, and her insides was all tore up like she'd been worked over by some maniac. I don't mind telling you, mister, I've seen some things in my time, but I don't want to see something like that again. There was bruises and cuts all over her body and one of her tits was half chewed off. The doc figures he must have been at her for a couple of hours."

'You say the girl was still alive?" Tom asked, puzzled. "Amos Wicklund told me she was dead when they found her."

"No, she was still breathing, according to Mr. Cartwright," Miles Townsend replied. "Maria lived long enough to tell him that it was Billy who did those things to her. Not that there was much doubt since he was found right there beside her and all. She died right afterwards, from internal bleeding, according to Doc Mayberry."

Tom Cavenaugh had been listening with increasing horror as the sordid story unfolded. Like Miles Townsend, he had seen more than his share of senseless violence directed against women and girls, things that made his mind reel at their sickening depravity. And it wasn't only Indians who could treat females that way. He felt his hands trembling as he tried to imagine his own brother turning into that kind of animal. It was true that men did change over the years. But he still couldn't bring himself to believe that Billy could do such monstrous things to another human being—one whom he supposedly loved. Townsend's voice brought him back to reality again.

"Billy was still passed out by the time I got out to Cartwright's house. Hell, he didn't wake up until the next morning. When he did finally come around he swore up and down that he didn't even remember going out to see the girl. He claimed he got drunk in one of the saloons and went back to the room he has in back of the feed store to sleep it off. I checked, of course, and he left the saloon before ten o'clock. He'd been drinking pretty heavy and got into a hassle with some cowboy who was teasing him about Maria. There wasn't no gunplay or even a fistfight, but Billy was acting pretty mean. My guess is that he went out to see Maria and, you know, he must have decided he was going to get some of that pussy or know the reason why. Maria must have said no and Billy went crazy. Anyway, the local magistrate charged him with rape and murder the next day and bound him over for trial.

I sent a message down to Prescott and asked whether they wanted to try him up here or down there. Judge Prescott was already on the circuit, so they decided to do it here. Look, Cavenaugh, I know how you feel over what's happened. But, believe me, the evidence was clear. Billy killed that girl. Shit, he wouldn't have done it if he was sober, I know that. It was the drink he'd had. Billy never could hold his liquor."

Tom Cavenaugh stood up and walked to the window, staring out into the darkness of Allison's main street. Townsend watched, wishing there was something he could do or say to make the other man's pain easier. When Tom turned and came back to the desk he was in control again.

"Tell me about last night," he said.

Miles told Tom that feelings had run pretty high in those first days after Maria's murder. Luckily, Maria's only relatives—two brothers, seemed unconcerned about their sister's death at the hands of a *gringo* and didn't cause any problems. And Townsend had warned everyone else that he would not tolerate anyone taking the law into his own hands. "I sure didn't figure anything would happen," he said guiltily.

"That leaves the most important question," Tom said slowly, his anger rising again. "Why was Billy left alone here at the jail?"

Townsend was uncomfortable as he tried to rationalize his own behavior of the previous evening. "Mr. Cartwright asked me out to dinner," he began. "He wanted to talk to me about taking on the job of town marshal. The town's big enough to have a local marshal instead of a deputy sheriff now. I didn't see any reason not to go. Hell, things were quiet enough and all the lynching talk had died out. I went out to the Cartwright's place about seven o'clock. The preacher's boy came out and told me what happened around eight-thirty. I came back to town right away but it was too late . . . Billy was already dead. They'd left him hanging there and went back to their goddamned drinking! Jesus, I couldn't believe it. I talked to everyone around, believe me. Not a damned soul would tell me anything . . . who was there, who put the rope on him, whose idea it was . . . not a goddamned blessed thing!"

He shrugged helplessly.

"I've been friends to every man in this town, but not a damned one of them would tell me a thing," he repeated in frustration.

"What about a man named Gilman . . . or Hilman?" Tom asked.

"J. R. Gilman?" Townsend asked, surprised. "He's foreman for the Conroy Ranch over by Ash Fork. What about him?"

"Tell me what he looks like . . . and whether he was in town last night," Tom demanded. He nodded as Townsend described the man. The description fit perfectly the one that cowboy Lacey had given Tom that afternoon.

"He and some of his boys were in town last night," Townsend went on, suspiciously. "Do you know something about him that I don't?"

"No, it's just a name I heard," Tom lied. "Where's my brother now?"

"I had him buried this morning," Townsend replied, bothered by the obvious lie. "The cemetery is about a mile out at the north end of town. Reverend Simmons from the Baptist Church said words over Billy."

He didn't add that he had paid for the simple burial from his own funds, or that the local undertaker had wanted to delay the burial long enough to exhibit the body at two-bits a customer, offering to share the proceeds with Townsend. "Listen, if you know something about J. R. Gilman you'd better tell me. He's a mean bastard and I'd like nothing better than to find out he had a hand in the lynching."

Tom ignored the question.

"What are your plans, Cavenaugh?" Townsend went on. "You're welcome to bunk in here if you want."

The thought of sleeping in the same jail from which his brother had been taken and murdered made Tom's stomach churn with agony. He shook his head. "Thanks, but I'll use the hotel. Where are my brother's things?"

Townsend got up and went to a pine cabinet by the wood stove. Opening it, he took out a neatly wrapped parcel. "This is all he had except his horse and saddle. Those are over at the livery stable." He paused, pointing to a neatly folded sheet of paper on top of the parcel. "I found that letter in Billy's cell this morning. I was going to send it to you. I don't know when he wrote it."

Laying the bundle on the sheriff's desk, Tom unfolded the letter, reading it slowly:

> Dear Brother Tom:
> They are fixing to try me for a crime which I did not commit, brother. I swear on the graves of our dear parents that I did not do that thing to Maria. If they hang me, Tom, pray for my soul. I know I done many things which made you ashamed of me, but I never did that thing to my darling Maria. We was fixing to get married and start a new life in California, but I never could stop drinking long enough to save no money. Reverend Simmons comes to see me every day and he says if I am innocent God will know it and reunite me with our parents and Maria in heaven. Sheriff Townsend is a good man too and tells me to be brave and face things like a man but I am afraid, dear brother. Come and see me if you can, brother.
>
> Your brother,
> William Everett Cavenaugh

Almost overcome with grief again, Tom refolded the letter and put it in his pocket. "When are you leaving Allison, Cavenaugh?" Miles Townsend asked.

"When I find the bastards who framed my brother and the ones who lynched him," Tom answered coldly, picking up the parcel and turning to leave.

Townsend came around the desk and stopped Tom before he reached the door. "Wait a minute, son," he ordered. "U. S. marshal or not, you've no authority here in Allison, and I won't stand for any more killing. Nobody framed Billy. As for the men who lynched your brother, well, I'll handle them myself without any help from you. Take my advice and ride out of here without giving me any problems."

Tom's eyes did not waver as he faced down the burly deputy.

"I gave up my star when I heard about Billy," he told Townsend. "I'm a private citizen and, by Jesus, I'll come and go as I please. You were kind enough to give me some advice, mister, so I'll return the favor. Don't interfere in my business unless you catch me breaking the law. Is that clear enough for you?"

"Clear enough," Townsend sighed. There was no point in saying any more at the moment, he knew. Tom Cavenaugh would do as he pleased, he told himself, and I'll do what I have to do. A confrontation between them seemed inevitable.

Tom left without speaking again.

He found the cemetery easily enough. There was a full moon and the night was still and beautiful in the soft light. A low rail fence surrounded the mounded graves with their small wooden crosses. Billy's grave was in a remote corner, apart from the others, as if his remains were too contaminated to rest with the more respectable citizens. It was only a mound of newly-turned earth covered over by a pile of rocks and with a tiny slab of pine giving his name and yesterday's date.

Kneeling beside the grave, Tom's eyes filled with tears as he made a silent vow to avenge his brother's death. He was not a religious man, so he said no prayer. He stayed there a long time, remembering the good times, grateful that their parents were not alive to suffer Billy's ignominious fate. Finally, standing, he muttered a final good-bye and turned to go, a cold hatred burning in his heart for the men who had done this.

Back in town, he checked into the cheapest hotel after making arrangements for stabling his horse. A quick meal followed, then a leisurely smoke on the hotel's wooden porch. The wind had come up, bringing with it cool air from the nearby mountains. Restless, knowing he would be unable to sleep even though he was bone-weary, Tom got his leather coat from his room and then went out to inspect Allison.

Tom liked to know an opponent, if possible, and this town was his opponent now. It would be a good time to take stock of Allison, to see what he was up against, to put the community into some sort of perspective. He began walking, mentally cataloging everything he saw. It was, he found, a prosperous town that had grown from a stage station to a community in less than five years. It still had a rawness to it, and buildings were still going up to house the new residents and businesses. To the west were silver mines. To the south were the plentiful and rich grazing lands of the broad Sweetwater Valley, with ample water and timber to supply the community's needs. And, if the railroad selected Allison for the north-south route, the town's future would be assured. If not, the town might slip back into oblivion when the mines ran out.

There were two churches, five saloons—not counting the small Mexican *cantina*, a weekly newspaper, a new feed store, several well-stocked general and specialty emporiums, the bank, a land office, the assay office, and several buildings housing the local attorneys and its single doctor. The town's whorehouse stood apart from the rest of the community on the western edge of town. All in all, Tom thought, Allison was probably a pleasant enough place to live and work.

But it was also the place where his brother had died, he told himself, and someone was going to pay for that cowardly act.

He passed no one on the streets as he completed his tour. By the time he was back where he started, he felt the need for a drink. Tom chose the noisiest and most garish of the three nearby saloons—the *Grubstake Bar*. It was almost nine o'clock when he went up onto the board sidewalk and pushed open the doors of the saloon. Card tables and other gambling paraphernalia took up one side of the large room, with a huge mahogany bar running the length of the other side. There were about two dozen men inside, equally divided between the gaming tables and the bar. A player piano stood at the far end of the saloon tinkling out the raucous notes of some sprightly tune currently in vogue.

Only a few of the customers looked up as Tom came inside and made directly for the bar. He chose the near end where he could have privacy but a good view of the others.

"Howdy," an overweight bartender said, leaving a group of men further down the bar to serve Tom. "What'll it be, mister?"

"Whiskey," Tom told the man, throwing a silver dollar on the polished surface. When the bartender returned with the bottle and a glass, Tom told him to leave the bottle. The man nodded, making a mark on the label with a pencil stub. The piano had stopped now. Tom waited a moment and then looked at the bartender. "I understand you lynched a man here last night," he said loudly enough so that everyone looked over at him.

The bartender nodded nervously without speaking.

"I didn't hear you," Tom went on in a flat, insistent voice. "What did you say?"

"There was a fella lynched last night but I don't know nothing about it," the bartender stammered, looking around at the other customers as if expecting some help from them. "Honest to Christ, mister, I was home sick in bed for two days. I didn't even *hear* about it until this morning."

"News travels slow in Allison, eh?" Tom asked sarcastically. "I would have thought everybody in town would have heard the poor bastard screaming and pleading for mercy." He looked around at the other customers. "Did *any* of you hear about it? Or were you all home sick in bed?"

No one answered.

"Now, I find that a little strange," Tom went on. "A mob of goddamned cowards drags a man out of jail and strings him up less than a hundred yards from here and nobody saw or heard a thing, is that it? What is it, are you assholes all deaf and dumb?"

A tall, lean youth stood up from one of the card tables and came toward the bar, a half-sneer on his face. His left hand rested easily on the gunbutt in the holster at his hip. He stopped in front of Tom, sizing him up. The youth was dressed in faded jeans and a dirty cotton shirt and appeared to be in his early twenties.

"What's your game, mister?" he asked with a hint of amusement in his voice. "How come you're asking about the lynching? You got some interest in that fucker we strung up?"

"My name is Cavenaugh . . . Tom Cavenaugh," Tom said quietly. "The man they lynched was my brother."

The young cowboy smiled.

"Jesus H. Christ, boys, don't this beat all? This feller says he's Billy's brother. He's come looking for the ones that kilt his brother, I bet." He paused, his eyes running over Tom's face insolently. "Yes sir, there's a resemblance all right, boys. What are you going to do to them fellers when you find 'em, mister?"

Tom ignored the question, asking one of his own.

"I've told you my name," he replied, trying to keep his voice calm. "Tell me yours, cowboy?"

"Why, sure, mister," the cowboy laughed. "I got *three* names . . . mean, bad-assed, and ugly! You just call me bad-ass for short, mister, when you apologize for them insulting things you said about us . . . you know, how we was *cowards* and *assholes.*"

"Were you one of them that lynched Billy?"

"Well, now, that's for me to know and you to find out, ain't it, Mr. Cavenaugh? I'll tell you this, though. That sure was a pretty sight to see your murdering brother jumping around on the end of that rope, wasn't it, boys? Some of the boys wanted to cut off your brother's balls before we swung him. That's what men should do to a sidewinding fucker who'd rape some poor little thing like Maria and then kill her."

"Carl, for God's sake, shut up," the bartender pleaded.

"Keep out of it, you fat piece of shit," the man named Carl growled. "What about it, mister? You think we should have sliced off his nuts before we strung him up?"

The bartender signaled frantically to one of the men at the bar. "Go get Sheriff Townsend," he ordered. The man started for the door when Carl's voice stopped him.

"Stay where you are," he insisted. "We don't need no law in this . . . any more than we needed the fucking law last night. The rest of you might be afraid of this dude, but I ain't." He turned his attention back to Tom Cavenaugh, the sneer still on his lips. "I always heard that bad blood runs in a family. The way I figure it, that don't make you any better than your goddamned murdering brother, mister. I'd sure watch my step if I was you or you might end up like Billy did."

Tom's hand came up involuntarily to caress the scar tissue on his forehead. Inside he was burning with rage but, outwardly, he appeared calm.

"I appreciate your concern for me," he said quietly. "Answer me, Carl, did you help lynch Billy?"

"I put the goddamned rope around his neck, mister," Carl boasted foolishly. "What do you think of . . ."

Carl's mistake was in watching Tom's hand massaging his forehead instead of staying alert. He didn't have time to finish the sentence before he felt a fiery pain down in his groin. It seemed as if his whole genital area was exploding. His right hand went instinctively toward the butt of his gun as he opened his mouth to scream out his agony. He was vaguely aware of Tom Cavenaugh's knee coming away from his groin, but there was no relief from the excruciating pain. Suddenly, his fingers only inches from the gun, he felt his breath driven from him by a savage blow in the stomach. Stunned, Carl flew backwards, knocking over a table and landing in a tangled heap on the floor.

Tom was on the cowboy before he could recover. He pulled the man's gun from his holster and sent it skidding across the floor out of reach. Then, using the back of his bandaged left hand, he battered Carl's face while his right hand pumped back and forth like a piston, turning the cowboy's face into a bloody mass of raw meat.

No one in the saloon made a move to help the cowboy.

All the pent-up rage Tom felt was suddenly directed against the moaning youth on the floor. He was oblivious to the pain in his left hand, feeling only an insane need to punish the cowboy for his taunting words. Unable to defend himself, Carl tried desperately to kick at Tom with his boot heels. The movement only enraged Tom all the more.

The fat bartender had scrambled around the bar and stood a few feet away, screaming at Tom. "For the love of God, mister, stop before you kill him!"

Suddenly Tom came to his senses. Wearily he climbed to his feet, panting hoarsely as he looked down at the cowboy. Carl was groaning loudly, holding his wounded genitals with one hand while he used the other to try and crawl out of range of Tom's boots.

He screamed in fear when Tom leaned down and dragged him to his feet, jerking him over to the bar and propping him there. Tom picked up the man's gun from the floor and forced it into the cowboy's hand.

"I'm going to give you one more chance than you gave my brother," he roared. "I'm going to count to three, you bastard. Either use that gun or crawl out of here on your fucking hands and knees like the miserable sonofabitching coward you are!"

He backed away, facing the cowboy. Those in the direct line of fire scurried to safety. The bartender pleaded with Tom to stop, then moved aside himself when he saw it was no use.

"One . . ."

Carl seemed too stunned by his pain to understand what was happening. He groaned again, jerking his head around pleading silently with the other men in the saloon for help. His testicles were still on fire, his knees threatening to collapse at any moment.

"No . . . don't . . ." he mumbled. "I don't want to fight you . . ."

"Two . . ."

Tom's hand was poised a few inches from his own gun, steady as a rock. His eyes narrowed as Carl's gun came up slowly, waving back and forth as the cowboy tried to control his aim.

Suddenly, with a cry of surrender, Carl let his body drop to the floor. The gun fell from his fingers and lay beside him. There was no fight left in him, only the desperate need to relieve the great waves of pain which were making him sick to his stomach.

"Crawl!" Tom ordered, nudging the youth with his booted foot. "Go on, crawl, damn it!"

Every inch was agony, but the cowboy finally managed to pull himself across the sawdust-strewn floor toward the door, moaning loudly and wincing as he went.

When he paused after a few feet, Tom came up beside him and drove the heel of his boot into the cowboy's tailbone, bringing a new shriek of misery from the other man's blood-flecked lips.

"Keep moving!"

The only sounds in the saloon now were from Carl's labored breathing as he struggled to reach safety. Tom followed, prodding with his boot, ready to drive the sharp tip into the other man's body again if he stopped.

Carl managed somehow to reach the door and push it open. Then, with a final effort, he propelled himself out onto the board sidewalk and lay there, gasping for breath. Tom stood over him in the doorway for a moment watching, a grim smile on his lips. When he spoke, his voice was full of fury.

"If I ever see your face again, I'll put a bullet through your goddamned heart, mister," he warned. "And, make no mistake about it, I'll be looking for you starting tomorrow morning, understand?"

The pain-wracked cowboy nodded, then began scrambling away.

The bar was still deathly quiet when Tom came back in and poured himself another drink. Downing it, he slammed the glass on the bar and turned to face the silent men.

"I'm giving fair warning to this whole town, starting with you, gentlemen," he told the nervous faces. "Anyone who had a hand in my brother's death is going to pay dearly for it. Hell won't be hot enough to hold the murdering bastards. I want you all to spread the word."

He went toward the door, then stopped and turned around.

"Where can I find a man named J. R. Gilman?"

No one answered for a moment. Then, finally, an elderly man pushed himself away from the bar and addressed Tom. "You might try the whorehouse, mister," he said. "J. R. and some of his boys were headed over that way a little earlier tonight."

"I'm obliged," Tom replied, nodding.

"No need to be, son," the man said, shaking his head sadly. "J. R. and that Conroy bunch will chew you up and spit you out like wormy meat after what you did to Carl Conroy. J. R. works for the boy's father and I wouldn't give a plugged nickel for your chances when they find out you snookered Carl like that. No, sir, you'll be out in the cemetery alongside your brother by this time tomorrow, and that's a fact, mister. I figure you might as well go and get yourself kilt quick and leave the rest of us in peace."

"That remains to be seen," Tom said, smiling grimly.

He went outside, pausing on the porch long enough to hear the excited buzz of voices inside. By morning everyone in Allison would know he was in town, and those who had a hand in lynching Billy would be looking over their shoulders and listening for his footsteps. That suited Tom just fine. Let them sweat, he thought bitterly, going out into the dirt street and moving toward the whorehouse. His wounded hand throbbed painfully and he cradled it against his stomach to ease the pain as he walked. Having only one good hand might be a disadvantage to some, but Tom had overcome handicaps much worse over the years.

He had passed the whorehouse on his earlier inspection of Allison and in five minutes he was standing in front of the unimposing building which housed the bordello. It was two-storied, constructed of raw pine with the ornate facade painted a pale blue color, and with a gold-lettered sign over the door announcing that this was the *Shady Lady* and that "Gentlemen" were welcome. About two hundred yards separated the *Shady Lady* from its nearest neighbor—a cheap roominghouse.

Tom was disappointed to find only one horse tied to the hitching post in front of the building. It seemed unlikely that he would find J. R. Gilman here tonight. He decided to go in anyway on the off chance that Gilman and his men might have stabled their horses and walked over to the whorehouse.

Heavy red velvet drapes were drawn across the downstairs windows, keeping out any prying eyes, but Tom could see the faint glow of lights inside. He pushed open the doors and found himself in the large foyer. Through the open doorway to his left he could see the large barroom with its polished mahogany counter and backbar. A huge oil painting of a reclining nude looked down on the room's only occupant, a bored and elderly negro bartender. The poker, dice, chuck-a-luck, and blackjack tables stood unused. To his right was the parlor. He strode over and looked inside the room. Two half-naked whores were playing cards on an ornate setee while they waited for customers. The room was large and garishly decorated, with overstuffed couches and chairs scattered around. Everything was decorated in striking reds and purples, giving the room a bizarre cast in the hissing light of the kerosene lanterns.

It was obviously a slow night for the whores.

One of the whores, a frowzy blonde, looked up and smiled at him. "Hi, honey," she called out. "Come on in, lover, we won't bite you." The other prostitute, a thin brunette with a pockmarked face, winked at him and put down her cards.

Suddenly Tom heard footsteps behind him and he turned to find himself staring at a barrel-chested man of about forty. The man's head was shaven clean and he wore a large, handlebar mustache above his thick lips. A tough customer, Tom thought, seeing the rippling muscles of the man's shoulders and arms through the silk shirt he wore.

"Evening," Tom said. "I heard J. R. Gilman was here tonight."

"He was, but he left an hour or so ago," the man replied, looking down at Tom's gunbelt. "If you're going to stay, you'll have to check your guns, same as everybody else, mister."

"Do you know where I might find him?" Tom went on, making no move to remove his holster. The bald man was obviously the bordello's bouncer. Tom had no doubt he was very good at his job.

"Back at the ranch, I suppose," the man replied. "What about it, mister? You staying or leaving? Things are pretty slow tonight, so you've got your choice of the ladies."

Tom had no real interest in anything the whores could give him except information. He looked back at the two whores who were now watching him with interest, wondering if it were worth talking to them. He decided it would be. "Sure, why not," he said, unbuckling his gun and handing the holster to the bouncer. The man hung the holster on a wooden rack in the foyer and handed Tom a brass check. "I'm Dave," he said, smiling for the first time. "You'll find the ladies clean, the tables honest, and the whiskey only about half water. You're a stranger, so I'll tell you our rules. We've only got a couple . . . no rough stuff with the girls and you pay in advance. What's your name, mister?"

"Tom is good enough," Tom said. "Are those two the best you've got to offer?"

"Irma and Sally ain't that bad, mister," Dave laughed. "But, no, most of the better ladies are upstairs resting since things are so quiet tonight. I'll send three or four of them down so you can look them over. The price is the same for all of them . . . three dollars a crack or ten dollars for the night. Except for Miss Louise, of course . . . she's five dollars and fifteen for the night. Take my advice and spend the extra money, mister. Miss Louise is well worth it."

"All right, send her down," Tom agreed. For the extra money there had to be something special about Miss Louise, he thought. He hoped it was worth it. "I'll be in the bar," he said as the bouncer went up the stairway toward the second floor.

Tom ordered a whiskey from the elderly negro barman while he waited. After he had been served he brought up the subject of J. R. Gilman. "You a friend of his?" the man asked. When Tom shook his head, the man seemed relieved. "He's a mean sonofabitch, mister, and I sure hate to see Mr. Gilman and his boys come in here at all. Mr. Dave throws them out regular when they get to raising hell or mistreating one of the ladies. They always come back, though."

Tom got no chance to ask any further questions of the barman. Hearing footsteps behind him, he turned. A tall, regal looking woman who appeared to be in her middle-thirties was coming through the doorway toward him, a dazzling smile on her lovely face. She was dressed in an expensive silk gown that left nothing to the imagination. Long black hair framed her delicate face with its deep-set dark eyes and full, pouting lips.

She looked like no whore Tom had ever seen, and she would not have been out of place in one of the balls at the territorial governor's mansion.

"Hello, Marshal Cavenaugh," she said, a teasing sparkle in her eyes.

Tom was shocked to be called by name. As far as he was aware, he had never seen this lovely woman before, although there was something faintly familiar about her. Embarrassed, he colored slightly as he nodded.

"You don't remember me, do you?" she laughed. When Tom reluctantly admitted that he didn't, the woman looked toward the negro barman and told him to bring drinks for them both, then took Tom's hand and led him over to one of the corner tables. The touch of her flesh against his own was exciting, and he wracked his brain trying to remember who she might be. When they were seated across the table from one another with their drinks—bourbon for Tom, champagne for her, she laughed again. "Don't look so guilty for not remembering me, Marshal Cavenaugh. It was a long time ago when we met, and under *very* different circumstances."

"Give me a clue," he begged. "It's hard to believe that I could forget someone as beautiful as you are."

"It was in the *Ace In the Hole Saloon* in Tucson . . . ten years ago," she teased. "As it turned out, the place was aptly named. My late husband was unfortunate enough to have been discovered with an *extra* ace in a high-stakes game there one afternoon. You saved him from being killed by three or four rather irate players who were going to shoot him. Surely you remember Carney Ferguson?"

Carney Ferguson! It all came back to Tom in a rush. He hadn't thought of the gambler or his wife in years. He looked at the lovely woman, shaking his head in wonder as he thought back to that day. Ferguson was one of the smoothest cardplayers Tom had ever seen. He and his young wife traveled from one town to another, staying long enough to fleece as many unwary victims as he could before common sense and outraged losers dictated they should move on. Tom had been drinking in the Tucson saloon that afternoon when Carny Ferguson, in a rare display of clumsiness, had let the extra ace fall from his sleeve to the floor. All hell had quickly broken loose, with three of the other players drawing down on Ferguson and about to shoot the gambler when Tom intervened. Stepping between them, Tom arrested Ferguson on the spot, then forced the other men to back down. After a quick trial, Carny Ferguson had been sentenced to three years in Yuma Prison for his trouble. As he recalled now, neither Carny nor the wife had thanked him for saving the gambler's life in return for one of the worst prisons in the country.

"Well, I'll be damned!" he said, shaking his head. "You say your husband is dead now?"

"Carney died two years ago in San Francisco," she

nodded. "After he was sentenced to Yuma Prison, I quickly discovered there was only one way to support myself. It's an old story, Marshal Cavenaugh. I worked in a whorehouse in Yuma waiting for Carny to be released, then we headed over to California and ended up in San Francisco. Carny was a broken man after what he'd gone through in that hell-hole, so I continued to work. A few years later I owned a house of my own . . . one of the best in San Francisco. Carny hated what I was doing, but the life suited me well enough. Two years ago Carny died of consumption."

"What are you doing in Allison?"

"Oh, there was a minor scandal involving some important politicians . . . one of whom was married to the daughter of the governor. I had to leave in rather a hurry, as you can imagine. I was on my way back east by stage and we stopped overnight here in Allison. The town was just starting to grow then and it didn't have a bordello . . . just a dirty little Mexican place. I had plenty of money, so I decided to open a place here. It's nowhere near as elegant as my place in San Francisco, but it suits me, and we do an excellent business most nights." She paused before going on. "You know, Marshal Cavenaugh, for a long time after you had helped send my husband to prison, I swore I'd shoot you if I ever saw you again. Oh, I know, you saved Carny's life, but I'm not sure it wouldn't have been kinder to let him die there in Tucson rather than suffering the way he did afterwards."

"I didn't see it that way," Tom replied nervously. He wondered if the beautiful woman carried a derringer. For all he knew one could be pointed at him under the table as she stared at him now. "Look, Miss Ferguson, I did what I had to do."

Suddenly she smiled again.

"Don't worry, Marshal Cavenaugh," she laughed, "I got over all that years ago. In a perverse sort of way, you did me a favor. Despite how they brutalized him in prison we had a few good years left together . . . and I'm a moderately wealthy woman now. If Carny would have died in Tucson, God only knows what would have happened to me. Shall we let bygones be bygones, then, Marshal Cavenaugh?" She lifted her champagne glass in a toast. "By the way, I'm no longer Sally Ferguson. People know me as Louise Lamour here in Allison. An appropriate name for the madam of a bordello, don't you think?"

"*You're* Miss Louise?" Tom asked, confused. "I didn't think most madams took on customers."

"Most madams are old hookers who hate men," Louise laughed. "I rarely turn tricks anymore, Marshal, but I've been feeling . . . how shall I put it . . . *restless,* lately. I asked my assistant Dave to keep his eyes open for someone who might be *special*! Dave knows my type and he told me about you, Marshal Cavenaugh. Don't look so shocked. I have *my* needs, too, and not many men can satisfy them. I was quite surprised to come down and find you of all people. Oh, you've aged some, Marshal, but you're as handsome as I remember from Tucson." She blushed prettily. "I think I always had ambivalent feelings about you, Marshal Cavenaugh . . . hating you all those years and at the same time wondering what it would be like to spend a night in bed with you. As I said, it takes a special type of man to satisfy me, Marshal . . . and I think it would be an experience you wouldn't soon forget. Would you like to come upstairs and talk about it?"

The wanton invitation excited Tom, there was no question of that. Over the years he had had more than his share of women . . . whores and respectable females alike. But none had possessed the incredible combination of beauty and sexual allure of the woman sitting across the table from him now. Besides, he told himself, if anyone in Allison could give him information on the town and its men, Louise Lamour was that person.

"I'd hate to disappoint you," he told her, already feeling the old familiar warmth of mounting desire in his loins.

She was already on her feet, smiling seductively. "You won't regret it, I promise you."

They passed the man named Dave in the foyer. Louise told him that she wasn't to be disturbed for the evening. Dave nodded, winking at Tom. "Goodnight, Miss Louise . . . Tom," he said, smiling.

Louise's spacious quarters were in a separate wing of the building, at the rear, and were as tastefully furnished as the rest of the house was garish. She poured drinks for both of them and then led Tom into the bedroom and sat on the huge bed watching him begin to take off his clothing.

"I forgot to ask you why you're in Allison, Tom," she said. "Just passing through? And what in God's name did you do to your hand?"

"The man these sonsabitches lynched last night was my brother Billy," Tom said as calmly as he could.

"Billy Cavenaugh was your *brother*?" Louise gasped. "Oh, Tom, I didn't know. How awful for you." She jumped up from the bed and put her arms around him, holding him close, trying to comfort him with her body. "I can't tell you how sorry I am, honey. Maybe this isn't a good time for us to . . . you know . . ."

"What I need right now is something to let me forget for a few hours," he told her, reaching around to undo the hooks of her dress. "Afterwards we can talk, if you don't mind. I've got a pretty good idea of who got that lynch mob all stirred up, but there's so much more about the whole damned thing that I don't understand."

"I'll do anything I can to help, Tom, you've got to believe that," she whispered. "Oh, God, if only I would have known Billy was your brother . . . I could have helped him . . ."

Her voice trailed off as Tom put one finger to her

lips and stopped the words. "Later," he said, "we'll talk later."

Tom climbed into bed while Louise undressed. She enjoyed disrobing in front of an appreciative man. And Tom was that, she could see. His eyes roamed over her lush flesh, taking in the soft swell of her breasts and then moving down to the flaring hips and thatch of curly pubic hair. He was already getting hard, she noted with satisfaction. She started to turn down the lamp, then decided against it, wanting to enjoy the sight as well as the feel of his hard-muscled body. Then, climbing in beside him, she let her slender fingers tangle in the mass of dark hair on his chest as the vibrations of warm passion surged through them both. "I want you," she whispered, her lips half-parted, her eyes glimmering with lust. "I want everything you've got . . . I want you to make love to me like you've never made love to any other woman."

Her hand moved down between his lean thighs where his penis was now hard and throbbing. She massaged it slowly, artfully, moaning with pleasure when his own hand began to run down gently over the naked velvet of her shoulders and then down to the softness of her buttocks. When his lips came down to kiss the ripeness of her tingling nipples, Louise shivered, never letting go of his manhood, teasing it with her nimble fingers until he was in a frenzy of lust. She gave a cry of joy when he pushed her down on her back and began stroking the entire length of her moistened, hair-lined furrow, his thumb strumming her already swollen clitoris like a fine instrument, bringing her closer and closer to the ecstasy she needed. Her thighs squeezed provocatively around his hand in a lewdly inviting caress. "Now," she pleaded. "Oh, God, don't make me wait!"

She threw her lovely long legs wide to receive him and her glistening orifice was pulsating uncontrollably. Stretching her arms up to pull him atop her, she groaned at the hot touch of his flesh against her own.

Tom needed no urging. He drove himself far up into the gaping hot mouth of her vagina, feeling her warm, elastic muscles clamp down wetly on his bloated penis as it raced without hesitation or resistance up into her hungrily welcoming belly. When he paused for a moment to savor the extraordinary sensation of erotic excitement that was consuming him, Louise cried out in frustration and began thrusting herself up to meet him in an agonized quest for more of the delicious pleasure he was giving her.

Putting everything out of his mind but the beautiful whore beneath him, Tom began to fuck her as hard and as fast as he could, sawing in and out with strong, brutal strokes. With each cruel thrust Louise arched her body shamelessly and begged for more, letting herself be lifted from the mattress by the potent strength of their connected bodies. She moaned ceaselessly, lewdly writhing and twisting her hips and crotch, flailing her head from side to side in sensual abandonment.

The harder he drove into her the more she wanted. And if it hurt and bruised her, that made their love-making all the more exciting. She lost herself in the burning pleasure of his thick penis ramming in and out of the moistly steaming mouth that clutched at him as if he were more valuable than anything else in the world.

Tom marveled at how tight the woman's pussy was. He knew she must have had hundreds of men over the years, yet she felt almost like a virgin. Suddenly she pulled up her knees and locked her legs around his back, the shift in angle enabling him to sink his rampaging penis even deeper into the juicy slit. Louise's eyes rolled uncontrollably in her head and her face was a mask of lust-contorted desire. "Fuck me!" she screamed. "More! Give me everything you've got!"

When her wildly contracting vagina convulsed around his penis to signal the first explosion of her orgasm, Tom heard a shriek of animal-like joy, and he drove into her again, hard and deep, driving the breath from her body as his own climax came.

Their movements slowed for a moment and then he began to stroke into her again, not as urgently this time, giving her time to savor each deep thrust. Louise came again and again, sending tremors through her quivering flesh as she ground her wet pussy up to meet him. Time seemed to stand still for both of them. Nothing mattered now but their quest for more and more pleasure from one another's bodies.

All of the pent-up emotion Tom felt about his brother's murder was sublimated through the body of the beautiful whore, all of his frustration disappearing in their wanton gyrations on the soft bed. For the moment there was only the violence of unrestrained sex—and he could not seem to reach the ultimate and final satisfaction. After a long, long time Louise went limp under him. She lay there, her arms and legs spread wide, her eyes closed, an expression of ecstasy on her lovely face.

"I've never felt so wonderful in my entire life," she panted, pulling him down beside her, her movements so skillful that he remained inside her. Finding him still hard, she laughed, a low, throaty chuckle that made her look even more radiant. "Give me a minute to rest, lover, and then I'll show you a trick or two I learned in San Francisco."

Tom laughed, too. "Rest, hell!" he grinned, withdrawing himself long enough to pull her limp body around so that she was kneeling in front of him. He took his penis in his hand and pressed it against the upturned wetness of her crotch, holding it there for a moment then sliding it up between her buttocks, searching for the little rosebud like opening there. Louise moaned, twisting herself back toward him, shaking her two ripe half-moons lewdly.

He was just about to push forward when there was a muffled rapping on the door. "Oh, damn!" Louise cried out angrily. "I *told* Dave I didn't want to be disturbed!"

"Ignore it," Tom told her. "He'll go away."

"No, it must be important," she said, getting up and putting on a sheer silk wrap. She gave Tom a quick kiss on the cheek and told him she'd be back in a moment.

Tom watched her go into the adjoining parlor. He could hear voices—Louise's and Dave's, but he couldn't make out what they were saying. Then the door slammed shut and Louise came back into the bedroom, an expression of apprehension on her face.

"What is it?" Tom asked, alarmed.

"Problems, Tom . . . serious problems," she told him, sitting down on the bed beside him. "Did you have some trouble with Carl Conroy earlier tonight?"

Tom explained what had happened between himself and the young cowboy in the bar, adding what he knew about J. R. Gilman and how the Conroy foreman had inflamed the mob which had murdered his brother. "I didn't come out here tonight for pleasure," he went on. "I'd heard that Gilman and some of his men were here."

Louise looked more worried than before. "They came back," she said, "they're downstairs now. They'd started back to the ranch but ran into Carl. He told them something about you jumping and threatening to shoot everyone concerned with Billy's death. Dave told them you weren't here, but I guess they don't believe him. Oh, Tom, you've got to get out of here. Get dressed, honey, you can use my private entrance."

"The hell I will!" Tom scowled, getting out of bed quickly and dressing. His wounded hand hampered him, and he winced as he tried to button his jeans and pull on his boots. Suddenly he remembered that his gun was downstairs in the foyer. "Shit, I checked my gun with Dave," he groaned. "Have you got a gun, Louise?"

"Please, I don't want any shooting here," Louise begged.

Tom had seen her quick glance at the bedside cabinet and he pushed her aside, opening the top drawer. A Colt .45 revolver and a pearl-handled derringer lay atop a pile of silk underclothing. Tom took both, jamming the revolver into his waistband, the derringer into his back pocket.

"Where are they?" he asked hoarsely. "In the bar?"

"Damn you, Cavenaugh, I can't afford to have any trouble here," the beautiful madam cursed. All the affection she had felt for him a few moments before was gone now. Her eyes were hard and her face was drawn as she stared angrily at Tom. "Sheriff Townsend has threatened to shut down the *Shady Lady* if we give him any problems," she pleaded. "If you're determined to shoot someone, do it somewhere else, for God's sake!"

"I'll try, but I can't promise you anything," he told her. "Where does that private entrance of yours lead to?"

"Out back . . . by the barn," she said with a sigh of resignation, still angry, but sensing there was nothing more she could do or say to dissuade him. "I'll show you."

She got up and led him into the parlor. A door opened off the rear wall, next to a bookcase. Louise unlocked the door and pulled it open. Tom could see a wooden staircase and the dim shape of the barn outside.

"How many men are with Gilman?" he asked urgently.

"Five or six," Louise told him. She paused, pulling at Tom's arm. "Look, Tom, this is a fool's game you're playing. I know how you feel, but wait for a better time. You can't take on J. R. and that crowd alone. Please, honey, don't try it!"

He shook off her hand easily.

"You don't understand . . . and I haven't got time

to explain it to you. Those bastards murdered Billy! By Christ, they're going to pay for it!"

"All right, go on, then. You're not going to rest until you get yourself killed, too, are you? One Cavenaugh in the cemetery isn't enough, is it?"

"We'll talk about it another time," he said, moving her out of the doorway so he could get past.

"If you do live through this . . . which I doubt, you won't be welcome here," Louise said angrily. "Go on, get out!"

There was no time to spend arguing with the distraught and enraged woman, Tom knew. Nodding, his face grim, he went out onto the stairway and pulled the door closed behind him, hearing the key turning in the lock. The night air was cold and he shivered in his shirt-sleeves as he went down the stairs quietly, listening intently for any sounds. It stood to reason that others would know of Louise's private entrance, and he had no intention of being bushwacked by Gilman or any of his men.

When he reached the bottom of the stairway he hesitated for a moment, then slipped around the house toward the front. The Colt revolver was in his hand, the hammer cocked. When he got to the front he paused again, peering around the building. He could hear voices from inside now—angry voices—and could see five horses tied to the hitching rail. Moving quickly, he crept over to the horses. They whinnied softly at his approach. Tom spoke to them in a reassuring whisper, praying they wouldn't get skittish and give away his game. Fortunately, they did not. He pulled a worn Winchester rifle from the scabbard of the first horse and tucked it under his left arm. There was no way of knowing how many rounds were in the chamber. Tom could only hope that its owner kept the rifle fully loaded. He was tempted to release the horses, but decided against it, afraid that the noise would alert the men inside to his presence and lose the element of surprise he hoped for.

Tom still had no plan. His emotions demanded that he go in and confront J. R. Gilman and his gang of bloody toughs without delay, to shoot them down as cold-bloodedly as they had helped lynch Billy. He wanted desperately to have the satisfaction of seeing their faces when they realized they were about to die. But his more rational instincts told him to go slow. He would get his revenge, a voice in the back of his mind told him, and it would be sweet. But, that voice went on, simply gunning down Gilman and the others would be little better than murder—no matter what the justification.

He was torn by the conflicting emotions he felt. Suddenly, without warning, he heard a shot, then the screams of terror from inside the whorehouse. Shocked, he raced up onto the porch and peered through an opening closest to the area from which the shot had sounded. It was covered by heavy red velvet drapes, but there was space enough between them for him to see the bordello's barroom.

A group of scantily-clad whores huddled together at one side of the room, guarded by a cowboy. Louise and the negro barman were bending over a sprawled body on the floor. Tom recognized the downed man as Dave, the bouncer. Another man stood over them, a scowl on his face, a revolver in his hand. Tom hadn't a doubt that he was staring at J. R. Gilman. The description of Gilman given Tom by the cowboy on the trail that afternoon fit this man perfectly. Tall and well-muscled, Gilman's hat was pushed back on his head, and his unshaven features were highlighted by the hawk-like nose and thick lips.

It was obvious to Tom, even at this distance, that Dave was dead. A gaping wound in his stomach was spreading a scarlet stain around the powder-burned shirt. Tom strained to hear the muffled voice of Louise Lamour as she sobbed over her former employee.

"You bastard!" she screamed up at Gilman, tears streaming down her face. "You didn't have to kill him, damn you!"

"This house nigger of yours is next unless you quit lying to me, missie!" Gilman warned harshly, waving his weapon in the direction of the frightened Black man. "If we find that sonofabitch Cavenaugh upstairs, I might even burn this whole goddamned place down."

"He's gone, I swear it!" Louise pleaded.

"We'll see," Gilman laughed mirthlessly. Reaching down, he grabbed Louise's arm and jerked the madam to her feet. She tried to pull away, moaning with pain, but Gilman held her tightly. "I know the fucker was out here . . . and I know him and you was upstairs screwing," Gilman went on, sneering at her cries of pain. "What I can't figure out is why you're protecting him, bitch. You got any idea what old man Conroy is going to do when he sees what that bastard did to Carl? Well, by Jesus, it ain't going to go easy with you, whore!"

He turned and looked at the other cowboy.

"Emil, go see what in the hell is keeping the boys," he ordered. "They've had time to search the whole goddamned place by now. Tell 'em to get back down here."

The cowboy nodded and went out through the doorway into the lobby and then disappeared from Tom's view. Tom knew he had to do something quickly, before Gilman carried out his threat to shoot the terrified barman. He also realized that he would have no chance against five men together. If he was going to take them on, it would have to be one at a time or in small groups. And Gilman was as good a place to start as any.

Tom moved away from the window and over to the front door, cocking his pistol as he went. Somehow he would have to get through the lobby and into the barroom before Gilman knew he was inside the whorehouse. And, he knew, he would be in serious trouble if

Gilman's men came back downstairs while he was still in the lobby. So intent was Tom when he put his hand on the doorknob that he failed to see the man coming toward the whorehouse from the direction of town. Only when when one of the horses whinnied did he look up in surprise.

"Hold it right there, Cavenaugh?" the voice of Deputy Sheriff Miles Townsend ordered. "Who fired that shot I heard? And what the hell are you doing sneaking out of here?"

The sheriff stood at the bottom of the steps leading up onto the porch, his pistol in his hand. The gun was pointed directly at Tom.

"J. R. Gilman just shot Dave," Tom whispered hoarsely. "And, I'm not sneaking out, as you put it. I was just about to go in after him before he kills anyone else!"

Townsend looked skeptical, frowning.

"What kind of shit is that?" he asked. "Why would J. R. want to kill Dave?"

"I'll tell you if we can move away from here before he or one of his men hears us," Tom replied impatiently. Townsend hesitated for a moment, then nodded, waving Tom down off the porch and away from the building. When they were far enough away so they couldn't easily be overheard, Tom quickly explained what had happened—the fight with Carl Conroy in town, his coming out to the *Shady Lady*, then Gilman and his ranch hands returning.

"Goddamn!" Townsend cursed. "Why in the hell didn't you tell me Gilman was mixed up in the lynching? I warned you about taking the law into your own hands, Cavenaugh. Now a man is dead because of you."

"There'll be more dead unless we stop him," Tom protested. "Gilman has already threatened to shoot that old Black bartender next, then to burn down the building. He's alone in the barroom now with Louise and the whores . . . the rest of his men are upstairs searching for me. Come on, we can't wait any longer!"

"I'll take care of J. R. and his plug-uglies," Townsend said emphatically. "You get your ass over to the jail and wait for me there. We've got that little matter of you kicking the shit out of Carl Conroy to talk over. Go on, git!"

"You can't face the five of them alone, damn it!" Tom said. "He's already killed two men if you count Billy . . . he's not going to let you arrest him!"

"J. R. and his men don't scare me none," Townsend shrugged. "Go on, you get out of here."

Without waiting for Tom to leave, Townsend strode toward the whorehouse. In a moment he was up on the porch and going inside, leaving the door open behind him. Tom had no intention of leaving now. He followed quickly. As he neared the open doorway he heard Townsend's voice, then the angry response of Gilman.

"Put down that gun, J. R. You're under arrest."

"Fuck yourself, Townsend," Gilman replied. "You ain't arresting me!"

The shooting began almost immediately.

Tom heard the hysterical screams of the whores as he raced toward the door opening onto the barroom. He counted three shots, praying that they had been from Townsend's gun rather than from Gilman's. Just as he reached the doorway, Miles Townsend staggered out of the bar, almost knocking Tom to the floor. The deputy sheriff's gun hung limply from his hand as a stain spread quickly around the bullet hole in his left shoulder. Grimacing in pain, Townsend cursed loudly and pushed Tom out of the line of fire.

"The bastard shot me!" he said incredulously.

Suddenly there was the sound of running feet from the upper floor. A moment later voices were calling down to Gilman.

"J. R.?" the cowboy named Emil cried out. "What's going on?"

Tom swung around just as Emil looked in on the scene below him. Then there were other men at the top of the stairs behind Emil.

"Drop those guns, all of you!" Townsend barked, his voice filled with pain.

Then there was another voice from behind the cowboy who stood on the stairway, one Tom instantly recognized as Carl Conroy's.

"That's him, boys!" Carl screamed. "That's Cavenaugh! Shoot the fucker, Emil!"

Emil's gun came up instantly even as Townsend repeated his order. It was obvious that his words would have no effect on the cowboy. Tom took aim with lightning speed a split-second before Emil could fire. His bullet struck Emil in the chest, sending the man tumbling down the stairway. The other men on the stairway scurried for safety as Tom squeezed off another shot.

"Look out, Cavenaugh!" Miles Townsend cried out.

Spinning around, Tom saw Townsend drop to one knee, facing the door into the barroom where J. R. Gilman stood, the ranch foreman's gun in his hand. Tom marveled later at how fast Townsend was able to get off his shot. The lawman's aim was off, but the bullet that splintered the wooden doorframe was close enough to drive Gilman back.

Suddenly there was a shot from the top of the stairway, missing Tom's head by inches. Spinning around again, Tom fired in the general direction from which it had come. He came around quickly enough to see that his shot had missed.

"Cover me, Townsend," he whispered hoarsely. "I'm going up after those fuckers!"

Before the deputy sheriff could protest, Tom leaped for the open doorway that would take him out onto the front porch. The wounded lawman would have to cover both the barroom entry and the stairway, Tom knew, but their only chance was for him to take out Gilman, then to get upstairs and behind the others.

He raced to the window. Peering inside, he could see Gilman pressing himself against the wall beside the door into the lobby. Fortunately, Louise, the barman, and the whores were huddled in a terrified mass behind the bar. Tom could hear shots being fired inside the *Shady Lady* and he prayed that none of them hit Townsend. Grabbing his pipe from his pocket, he moved over to the next window and stepped back a few paces. Aiming the pipe at the other window, he threw it as hard as he could, hoping that Gilman would fire in that direction when he heard the noise.

As soon as he let go of the pipe, Tom raced back to the second window, holding his pistol by the barrel. Through the curtains he could see Gilman staring at the other window and aiming. A shot rang out, breaking the glass.

Hammering the unbroken window with the butt of his gun, he heard the glass splinter as Gilman swung around, a surprised expression on his face. Before Gilman could fire again, Tom managed to squeeze off a shot that caught the foreman in the groin. Gilman screamed and fell to the floor as his gun fell uselessly out of reach.

Racing back into the *Shady Lady*, Tom fired off two rounds in the direction of the top of the stairway. "Keep 'em busy," he yelled at Miles Townsend. The deputy nodded, although Tom could see that he was in great pain from his shoulder wound. Then, moving quickly into the barroom, Tom found J. R. Gilman unconscious but still alive, the man's jeans a mass of blood from the wound in his groin.

Several more shots were exchanged between Miles Townsend and the men at the top of the stairs. Breathing hard, Tom took time enough to discard his own weapon and grab up Gilman's gun, reloading it from the foreman's gunbelt.

"Louise! Get out here!" he yelled in the direction of the bar. In a second the madam's face was peering over at him from behind the mahogany counter. When she saw that Gilman was helpless, she stood up and joined Tom quickly. He pointed down at Gilman. "See if you can stop the blood! I don't want this bastard dying on me!"

When Tom went back out into the lobby he found Miles Townsend near unconsciousness. The lawman's gun was wavering when he tried to point it up at the men on the upper floor.

"Can you hold out for another five minutes?" Tom asked urgently. Townsend nodded, trying to smile. "Good! Gilman's down and I'm going to get the rest of those fuckers!"

Without waiting for the deputy sheriff to reply, Tom went back out the front door and around the building as quickly as he could. He took the steps up to Louise's private quarters three at a time, then raced out into the corridor that led to the main hallway which ran along the second story of the *Shady Lady*. Covering the twenty or so feet in record time, he skidded to a stop when he reached the end. Peering cautiously around the corner, he breathed a sigh of relief when he saw that all three men had their backs to him and were concentrating on Miles Townsend downstairs in the lobby.

"Throw down your guns and come down!" Townsend's voice came up at them.

The three ranch hands' answer was a volley of shots and obscenities.

"The first one of you bastards who moves is a dead man!" Tom cried out, stepping out into the hallway behind them. One of the men, a baby-faced youth didn't heed Tom's warning. He cursed and swung around to face Tom.

The top of the youth's head exploded in a shower of gore, hair, and skull splinters as Tom shot him, then turned his gun on Carl Conroy who had rolled to one side and come up on his knee.

"Drop it!" Tom shouted, his finger tightening on the

trigger of his weapon. Carl's face went white and his eyes went to the body of his dead companion. Slowly his grip on his revolver relaxed and the gun fell heavily to the floor.

"Don't kill me!" he pleaded hysterically.

The other man let go of his own gun at the same time. It clattered down the stairway and he raised his hands slowly. "Get up, both of you," Tom ordered. He watched them cautiously while he called out to Townsend, "Townsend! It's Cavenaugh! Hold your fire . . . I'm bringing them down!"

Jabbing Carl Conroy and the other cowboy in the ribs with his gun barrel, Tom forced them down the stairway. Miles Townsend had managed to stand up, but he was leaning against the wall for support.

"You'd better get the doctor out here," he moaned, his face ashen. "I don't think I can make it much longer . . ."

And then his eyes closed and he slid to the floor beside the body of the first of the Conroy ranch hands that had been killed in the exchange of gunfire.

Suddenly there were voices outside and a crowd of men streamed up onto the porch of the *Shady Lady*. Tom was shocked to see Amos Wicklund staring at him from the doorway. The U. S. marshal's eyes quickly took in the scene.

"Amos!" Tom gasped. "What are you doing here?"

Wicklund strode into the room, shaking his head in amazement. "I changed my mind about going back to Prescott," he replied, kneeling beside Miles Townsend and putting his handkerchief to the other man's wound to try and staunch the flow of blood. "I caught a few hours sleep and then followed you. Jesus, Tom, it looks like a slaughterhouse in here. What happened?"

Chapter Four

Tom Cavenaugh and Amos Wicklund didn't get the chance to sit down and talk until almost two hours later. First, there was the urgent matter of getting medical attention for Miles Townsend and J. R. Gilman, both of whom were losing blood at an alarming rate. A large crowd had followed Amos out to the *Shady Lady*, attracted by the sounds of gunfire. They were pushing and shoving one another now in an attempt to get inside the bordello so they could see the bloodshed at first hand.

Amos handled the mob forcefully, identifying himself as a U. S. marshal and threatening them all with arrest if they didn't disperse. He singled a half-dozen men out of the crowd, ordering one to go for the local doctor, another to go and awaken the undertaker, and the remaining to come inside and stand guard over Carl Conroy and the other ranch hand until they could be transported into the jail and locked up.

That done, Amos ordered Louise Lamour to take all the prostitutes upstairs and to remain there until he sent for them. The doctor arrived quickly—a cynical, elderly physician named Mayberry. He took in the scene without comment, then examined both men and put compresses on their wounds to stem the dangerous loss of blood. "I'll need a wagon to take them into my clinic," he told Amos. The undertaker had arrived soon after the doctor, and his rig was pressed into service for the job, with Tom and Amos helping to load the wounded men into the bed of the wagon.

As soon as the doctor and his patients were gone, Amos checked on the two prisoners and then led Tom into the barroom of the bordello. Dave's lifeless body still lay in the middle of the floor, a sheet draped over it. "You'd better tell me what happened, *amigo*," the marshal said, opening a bottle of whiskey and setting it on the bar between them.

Wearily, Tom went through the events since his arrival in Allison—the rage he had felt upon learning of his brother's death, the confrontation with Miles Townsend, the brawl in the saloon with Carl Conroy, his coming out to the *Shady Lady* in search of J. R. Gilman. Amos listened quietly, not speaking until Tom was finished.

"I'm sorry as hell about Billy," he said at last, his eyes full of sympathy for his friend. "It doesn't make a lot of sense, them lynching him like that when Judge Manners was on his way here . . . especially since Miles Townsend seemed to have things under control. Shit, when those things happen it's usually right off, not after tempers have cooled off."

"I think someone put those bastards up to it, Amos," Tom protested. "I think somebody wanted to make damned sure Billy was dead and buried before anyone could find out he was innocent of killing that girl!"

He told Amos about the letter from Billy, the one Townsend had given him earlier that evening. Amos listened, but he seemed unconvinced.

"Hell, son, from what you've told me, they had Billy dead to rights. I mean, face it, Tom, would you think he was innocent if he wasn't your *brother*? Every bit of evidence points to Billy and no one else!"

Tom refused to accept his brother's guilt, no matter what the evidence had been. "No, you're wrong,

Amos," he insisted hotly. "Billy loved that girl . . . he wouldn't kill her!"

Amos shrugged helplessly.

"Well, we'll talk more about it tomorrow," he said in resignation, pushing himself away from the bar. "I'm going to go up and talk to the madam and her ladies and get her version of what happened here tonight. There's going to be a hell of a ruckus over these three killings, and I don't want anybody saying you gunned down anybody out of revenge over Billy. Afterwards I'll go in and have a talk with Miles Townsend if he's conscious." He paused, staring at Tom as if trying to decide something in his mind. "Can I trust you to take those two prisoners in and lock them up?" He added, quickly, "It isn't that I don't trust you, Tom, but I know how high your feelings are running now."

Tom was stunned by the implication of the question, stunned and angry that Amos Wicklund of all people would think him capable of shooting unarmed men. Forcing himself to ignore the insult, he nodded.

"Good," Amos said. "Put 'em in a cell and then go get some sleep. We'll see if we can't figure this mess out in the morning."

Fifteen minutes later, Carl Conroy and the other cowboy—whose name Tom discovered was Will Hoffstader—were safely locked in their cells. The two had come along peacefully enough, but as soon as Tom had dismissed the men who had accompanied them, Carl Conroy began to tremble violently as Tom stared through the bars at him.

"Oh, Jesus, Will, he's going to kill us!" Carl screamed, backing to the far corner of the tiny cell and trying desperately to make himself into as small a target as possible. Will Hoffstader just stood and looked on from his adjoining cell, his face ashen with fear. "Please, mister, don't shoot me!" Carl moaned hysterically.

Tom had no intention of harming Carl Conroy or

Will Hoffstader, but this was too convenient an opportunity to miss. He was becoming more and more convinced that his brother's death had been no mere spur-of-the-moment act of bloodletting by a drunken mób. Amos had been right: Most lynchings came immediately after the crime had been committed, when passions were still inflamed, not almost two weeks later, with a judge on his way to conduct the trial! J. R. Gilman and his crew of thugs had been the instrument of Billy's death, he knew, but Tom was certain that the *idea* must have been someone else's!

He unlocked Carl's cell and stepped inside, locking it behind him. Wide-eyed, terrified, Carl moaned louder when he saw Tom coming closer.

"How badly do you want to live, Conroy?" Tom asked ominously.

"Please, don't kill me," Carl whined.

"I might be willing to forget your part in this business if you tell me who put Gilman and the rest of you bastards up to lynching Billy."

"It was J. R.'s idea . . . he made me do it," Carl cried out, his whole body shaking with terror. "Honest to God, mister, I didn't want no part of it . . . you've got to believe me!"

"That's not what you told me in the saloon tonight."

"That was just bragging on myself . . . I didn't want to help kill Billy . . . he never done me no harm! J. R. got me all likkered up and crazy with all his talk about what Billy done to Maria Gomez . . ." his eyes darted over to Will Hoffstader, ". . . you tell him, Will . . . tell him it wasn't my fault!"

Even Hoffstader seemed sickened by Carl's behavior. He looked back at Carl in disgust, shaking his head. "Nobody made you do nothing, you lying piece of shit!" he responded angrily. "Jesus, can't you act like a man for once in your life?"

"What about it, Conroy?" Tom went on. "Who put J. R. up to this business?"

"Keep your mouth shut, Carl!" Hoffstader warned. "Your daddy'll skin you alive if you tell him anything."

Tom let his hand come down to rest lightly on the butt of his gun. When Carl Conroy saw the movement he began screaming, sure he was about to be murdered.

"No! I'll tell you!" he shrieked. "Just don't shoot me, mister, please!"

"Spit it out, then, damn it! What has your father got to do with this? Is he the one who told Gilman to whip up that lynch mob?"

"Carl!" Hoffstader warned again.

But it was too late. Carl was beyond self-control. The words came tumbling out as he looked up at Tom with pleading eyes.

"Daddy give J. R. fifty dollars and told him to take some of the boys into town and teach Billy Cavenaugh a lesson . . . he said the sheriff would be gone from the jail around seven o'clock and that we could . . . could . . ."

"Go on," Tom prompted.

". . . daddy told J. R. to use the money to buy drinks and get the folks riled up against Billy . . . oh, Jesus, mister, I'm sorry . . . I never seen a man kilt before . . ."

"What did you father have against Billy?" Tom asked hoarsely, his heart pounding heavily against his ribs. "Goddamn you, Conroy, tell me!"

"Nothing!" Carl screamed. "He didn't even know Billy! He was doing it as a favor to Mr. Cartwright and Jeb Fallon, I think! Them two was out at the ranch that afternoon talking to daddy before he sent us and J. R. into town! That's all I know, mister, honest to God!"

Shocked by what Carl had told him, Tom grabbed the front of the youth's shirt with his wounded hand and balled his right fist at the same time.

"What did they talk about? Tell me, you low-life sonofabitch or I'll kill you with my bare hands!"

"Something about seeing to it that Billy didn't get no trial!" Carl moaned piteously, expecting the first blow to land at any moment. "I walked in when they was talking . . . but daddy chased me out!"

The youth suddenly began sobbing wildly and hiccuping at the same time. Tom held his shirt for a moment and then, with a harsh sigh of suppressed rage, let go. He would get no more from Carl Conroy for the moment, he knew, even assuming that the man knew any more. Tom's mind was in a raging turmoil as he left the cell and went out into the sheriff's office. So Harold Cartwright and Jeb Fallon were behind the thing, he told himself. Maria Gomez's employer and one of the men who had found the girl that night had plotted to deprive Billy of his trial. But why? Was it simply their rage at the crime? That logic seemed to make little sense to Tom. If that was the case, why didn't they just shoot Billy when they discovered him in bed with the murdered girl that night? Surely their actions would have been more understandable in light of the heinous crime which had been committed. Instead, they had waited so long, and then found someone else to do their dirty work!

The clock on the office wall told him it was twenty minutes to three. Suddenly he was tired, more exhausted than he had been in months, too weary even to think straight. He badly needed a few hours sleep, and his business with the owner of the Conroy Ranch, Harold Cartwright, and Jeb Fallon would have to wait until he was refreshed.

Tom went out into the cool night air and crossed the dirt street to his hotel. Taking his key from the board behind the counter, he went upstairs and fell into bed without undressing. He lay there like that for a long time before he finally closed his eyes and let a merciful sleep carry away the ugly images that filled his mind.

* * *

Tom had counted on his mental alarm clock to awaken him at seven o'clock the next morning. For the first time in years the trick failed, and he found it was almost ten when he finally opened his eyes and sat up. Cursing, he quickly splashed water on his face from the pitcher and china basin on the dresser, then ran his fingers through his hair. He hurried downstairs, ignoring the stares of the clerk and customers in the lobby, heading directly for the jail.

Amos Wicklund was sitting behind the sheriff's desk when Tom entered. The marshal looked up and gave Tom a wry grin. "I was about to come over and wake you up, old son," he said, pointing toward the enameled coffeepot on the woodstove. "Get yourself some coffee and sit down."

The coffee smelled too good to resist. When he was seated across the desk from Amos, a cup of the strong black brew in his hand, he asked, "How's Miles Townsend?"

"The doc patched him up and says he'll be up and around in a week or so," Amos replied. "He didn't have as much luck with J. R. Gilman, though. He died about four o'clock this morning. No loss to the world, as far as I can see."

"Shit!" Tom exploded in frustration. "I had some questions for that bastard!"

"Yeh, our friend Hoffstader in there . . ." he pointed toward the back of the jail, ". . . told me about your little session with Carl Conroy last night. You must have scared Carl pretty bad to have him tell you all about his daddy and Cartwright and Fallon putting Gilman up to what he did."

"I *told* you someone else was behind the lynching!" Tom said angrily. "And I *told* you Billy was innocent. This proves it!"

"No, it don't, Tom," Amos replied calmly. "You're not thinking straight, son. All this proves is that old man Conroy, the banker, and Jeb Fallon had a talk the day Billy was killed. Carl didn't hear anything all that incriminating and, anyway, that boy would do or say anything to save his own ass. No, the one thing don't necessarily follow the other, *amigo*."

"But, damn it, Amos, that's the only way it makes any sense," Tom argued forcefully, struggling to keep his temper. "Why else would they want Billy dead?" He stood up, his patience at an end. "Ah, to hell with all this talk. I'm going out to the Conroy ranch and get the truth out of him."

"You'd be wasting your time," Amos said quickly. "He rode into town this morning looking for Carl and Gilman and the others."

"Where is he now?" Tom asked hoarsely, feeling the hair on the back of his neck standing up.

"Settle down, son," Amos told his friend. "When folks told him what had happened, he stormed in here and had a hell of a row with Carl and Hoffstader . . . threatened to shoot the both of them if they said one goddamned word to anyone before he could get them out of jail. Then he came roaring in here and screaming to me about all his high-powered friends down in Prescott, and how he was going to see the whole crowd of us in hell before he was done . . . you, me, Miles, and even that pretty whore friend of yours out at the *Shady Lady*. I told him what the boy had told you, but he denied the whole thing . . . said Cartwright and Fallon had come out to talk over a business deal they were involved in together. I swear, Tom, that old man is as mean and as dangerous as they come."

"Where is he now?" Tom repeated.

"He had a talk with Mr. Cartwright at the bank, then caught the stage for Prescott about an hour ago."

"Why didn't you hold him?" Tom demanded.

"On what charge? We don't have anything on Conroy yet, Tom. Don't worry, he'll be back. In the meantime, it'll give us a chance to nose around and see if we can find out what really happened the night the girl was killed. Look, son, I'm still not convinced your brother Billy was innocent. Maybe he was, maybe he wasn't. Why don't we approach this like any other investigation instead of you running off half-cocked and wanting to shoot everybody in sight? It seems to me that that's the way to clear your brother's name. Oh, by the way, since Deputy Sheriff Townsend is going to be laid up for a few days, the town council asked me to ride herd on things here until he's back on duty."

Tom poured himself another cup of coffee while he thought over what Amos had said. Maybe his friend was right, he told himself. Two of the men who had helped lynch Billy were already dead, two more in jail, and yet Tom didn't feel any satisfaction. Even if he avenged himself on every man in the lynch mob, Billy's guilt in the murder of Maria Gomez would still be assumed. Perhaps it *would* be better to put aside his personal feelings for the moment and act as if an unknown person—instead of his own brother—were the suspect. Could he be that detached, he wondered?

"What are you thinking?" Amos Wicklund asked.

"I'm thinking you may be right," Tom admitted reluctantly. "All right, Amos, I'll try it your way. Tell me, what are Conroy's chances of pulling any strings with the territorial officials in Prescott? Can he cause you or Miles Townsend any problems over what happened last night?"

"Hell no," Amos laughed. "It's an open and shut thing, as far as Miles and I are concerned. Gilman and the others killed that fellow at the cathouse, then resisted arrest and tried to kill Miles. No, there's nothing that Conroy can do to us. I don't know about Louise Lamour, though. If I was her, I'd think seriously about packing up and moving on. Why don't you get yourself cleaned up a little and then have something to eat, Tom? You look like something the cat dragged in.

Afterwards, we'll go back to the beginning and see whether we can find out if Billy really did kill the girl. Fair enough?"

"Fair enough," Tom replied, standing up again.

"One thing, though," Amos added. "I want your promise that you'll leave it to the law if we find that someone other than Billy killed Maria Gomez. Understood?"

It was the most difficult promise that Tom Cavenaugh had ever made, but he finally nodded his assent, praying that when the moment of truth came his word of honor would be more compelling than his burning need for vengeance.

It was almost one o'clock by the time Tom finished his bath, shave, and meal. He ate alone at a corner table of the hotel's dining room, and it was obvious from the way the other diners whispered to one another and stared at him that his presence was well-known in Allison. Even the elderly waiter seemed nervous when serving Tom's food.

He had a cigar after lunch, then walked back to the jail. Amos had Miles Townsend's reports on the girl's murder spread out on the desk, and they went over them carefully. When they were finished, an hour later, they both sat back in their chairs and stared at one another.

"What do you think?" Tom asked.

"I think we'd better go back and interview everyone involved," Amos replied. He tapped the reports with his finger. "Something bothers me here, but damned if I know what it is. I'll tell you what, you take Jeb Fallon and this fellow Marcus Owens for a start. I'll go after the banker and the girl's two brothers. Why don't we meet back here around six? We can have supper and talk."

The arrangement was agreeable to Tom, although he would have preferred to interview the banker himself. Saluting his friend, Tom went back out onto the street.

The sun was overhead now, and most of Allison's residents were sensible enough to be inside, out of the heat. According to Townsend's reports, Jeb Fallon owned the feed and grain store; Marcus Owens one of the town's general stores. Both establishments were within a block of one another just off the main street.

The general store of Marcus Owens was closed and shuttered when Tom arrived. A sign hung on the door announcing that it would reopen at two-thirty. Tom checked his watch and found he had ten minutes to wait. He was sitting in the shade of the porch when the heavy-set, middle-aged man came down the street toward him. The man was dressed in shapeless trousers, a white shirt, and an alpaca jacket. He was balding, with coarse features and a petulant expression on his lips. He was within a few feet of the porch when he noticed Tom. Surprised, he stopped abruptly, eyeing Tom nervously.

"You looking for someone, mister?" he asked warily.

"I'm looking for Mr. Owens . . . *Marcus* Owens. Would that be you?"

"What do you want?" the man nodded.

"I'm Tom Cavenaugh," Tom said, introducing himself, wondering why Marcus Owens would be so frightened of strangers. As soon as the words were out of Tom's mouth the man began to sweat and his double-chin started to tremble. He backed away from the porch rapidly.

"You get away from my store, do you hear me!" Owens cried out. "I ain't got nothing to say to you or your kind! And I didn't have nothing to do with lynching your brother, either!"

Owens looked around the empty street, desperately hoping to find someone to whom he could turn for help. When he saw no one, he turned and raced off in the direction from which he had come, raising the dust, leaving Tom standing there watching him disappear around the nearest corner.

"Well, I'll be goddamned!" Tom swore aloud, bewildered by the man's terrified reaction. After a few moments he shrugged and made his way to the feed and grain store in the next block. It was a long, two-storied frame building with double silos at the rear and a small office in the front. Unlike Marcus Owens' establishment, the door was open.

A sullen-looking youth of seventeen or eighteen sat at a small desk with a lurid dime novel propped in front of him. He looked up as Tom entered, but there was more annoyance on his face than interest.

"Is Mr. Fallon in?" Tom asked.

"He ain't here," the boy replied, turning his attention back to his book.

"When *will* he be in?" Tom asked impatiently.

The boy mumbled something incoherent.

Angry, Tom stepped closer and knocked the novel out of the surprised boy's hand, sending it flying across the small office. "Hey, what you doing!" the boy started to protest, his voice trailing off when he saw the expression on Tom's face.

"Look at me when I talk to you, son," Tom said coldly. "I asked you a question . . . when will Mr. Fallon be in?"

"Jesus, I don't know, mister. Charley Cummins . . . he's the foreman here . . . he said Mr. Fallon was taking his wife and daughter up to Ash Fork to visit her folks. Charley didn't say when he'd be back."

"When did he leave?"

"Early this morning, I guess . . . I don't know. He was here last night when I went home."

"Where would I find this Charley Cummins, then?"

The boy pointed in the direction of the rear of the building. "He's out back sleeping off his lunch."

The youth was picking his book off the floor when Tom went through the office door and out into the grain-drying shed. It took a few minutes, but he finally located Charley Cummins stretched out on several bales of hay. Cummins was a thin man in his mid-forties, with a consumptive look about him. He scrambled up quickly when Tom shook his shoulder.

"Yes, sir, be right with you," Cummins said, trying to smile as he shook off the sleep. Suddenly the smile was gone. "Hey, you're Mr. Cavenaugh, ain't you? I was in the saloon last night when you had that set-to with Carl Conroy. Jesus, is it true you killed J. R. Gilman and Emil Kinney out at the whorehouse after you left the saloon?"

Tom ignored the question.

"I understand Jeb Fallon left town this morning," he said. "Was this something he'd planned?"

Cummins grinned again, brushing the straw off his shirt and trousers. "It sure wasn't" he replied. "He and I both came in about six-thirty this morning. Well, sir, damned if I ain't the biggest gossip in town, and I couldn't wait to tell him about you showing up and half-killing the Conroy boy last night . . . then about the shoot-out at the *Shady Lady*. Jeb got all white in the face and made me tell him the whole story *twice*! Then, damned if he don't tell me he's taking his old woman and his kid up to Ash Fork right away, and that I'd have to run things here until he got back. He lit out of here like the devil was chasing him, Mr. Cavenaugh."

"Maybe he was planning the trip all along and just came to tell you," Tom suggested, not believing that explanation for a moment.

"No, sir, that couldn't be," Cummins answered, shaking his head. "Before I'd told him about you he had already said how he was going to spend the whole day going over the accounts." He paused, scratching his head. "He's been nervous as a cat ever since your bro . . . I mean, since the Gomez girl was murdered . . . him being right there when the body was discovered, and all. Shit, that'd make any man skittish, I reckon."

"Did Jeb Fallon know the girl?"

"Oh, sure, everybody in town knew Maria," Cummins grinned, rolling his eyes lewdly. "Hot damn! She sure was a sexy thing, Mr. Cavenaugh . . . the way those titties bounced when she walked, and her little ass shaking around like crazy! Jeb wasn't no different than the rest of us . . . he'd have give anything to get that little hot tamale to spread her legs for him."

"What about the girl's employer, Mr. Cartwright?" Tom asked cautiously. "You think he was fooling around with Maria?"

Charley Cummins chuckled obscenely.

"Everybody sure *thought* so," he nodded. "Jeb Fallon was always testing him about Maria and making out that Cartwright was trying to keep all the good-looking women in Allison to himself."

"I don't understand," Tom said.

"Hell, mister, Maria Gomez couldn't even hold a candle to Mr. Cartwright's wife Amy. Now there's *class* for you! Tall, blonde lady, hardly much older than Maria, but just about the most beautiful thing I ever saw in my life! It sure ain't no wonder Cartwright is so jealous of her. He'd just about go crazy if another man looked at Mrs. Cartwright, according to Jeb Fallon. And everybody in town knows how jealous Mr. Cartwright is of his wife. I was over at the bank one day when Mrs. Cartwright come in to see her husband for something. There was a drummer from St. Louis out in front of the bank when Mrs. Cartwright pulled up in her buggy. This dude made a big fuss about helping her down . . . you know, flirting and making up to her. Cartwright happened to come outside about then and he damned near had a fit. He run that drummer off and then lit into his wife . . . making out like it was her that was doing the flirting instead of the other way around. I felt sorry for the poor thing. She was in tears when I left."

Thank God for town gossips, Tom told himself.

"Do you think the banker had any reason to be jealous of his wife?" he asked, adding, "Or she of him?"

Charley Cummins started to answer, then stopped, as if he realized he had already said too much about the banker who was, after all, the richest and most powerful man in Allison. Tom tried again, but it was no use. Cummins begged off answering any more questions, saying he had to get back to work. "No," he said, "I don't know when Jeb is coming back."

Tom left, thanking the man. As he walked back toward the jail he passed Marcus Owens' store. Seeing the door open and the shutters pulled, he went inside. An overweight, greying woman stood behind the counter, waiting on a young girl.

"Is Mr. Owens in?" Tom asked politely. The store contained a dizzying mix of merchandise—with everything from miners' tools to household goods and groceries. With things stacked everywhere, it would have been easy to miss seeing the portly store owner.

"My husband took sick after lunch," the woman replied, eyeing Tom suspiciously. "If you're a drummer, you're wasting your time . . . we don't need nothing."

She was so unpleasant that Tom left without asking any further questions. It seemed uncommonly strange that two of the three men who had found the body of Maria Gomez had become so rattled by his arrival in Allison, with Jeb Fallon leaving town, with Marcus Owens taking to his sickbed. And then there was the matter of the banker and the dead girl, he told himself. Tom wondered if the local gossip had any truth to it—that Cartwright may have been sleeping with Maria Gomez on the side, even though he had a beautiful young wife of whom he seemed to be insanely jealous?

Tom looked at his watch and saw that it was not yet four o'clock. He had agreed to meet Amos at six. That left more than an hour to kill. He decided to go out and have a look at the murder scene. Perhaps there was something there that the sheriff and the others had overlooked, he told himself, something that might clear Billy's name. And it would give him a chance to meet the beautiful Amy Cartwright. Tom already knew that Mrs. Cartwright had been away on the night of the murder. Still, she might knew something about the relationship between Billy and Maria Gomez that might help Tom understand what had happened.

Since he had no idea where the Cartwright house was located, Tom has to ask directions from an elderly man sweeping the sidewalk of the nearby land office. The old man looked at Tom for several seconds before replying, then gave the directions. As soon as Tom had thanked him and started up the street again, the man threw down his broom and made for the nearest saloon to boast about actually speaking to the brother of Billy Cavenaugh. It was the most excitement the old man had had in months.

Amos Wicklund had decided to speak to the two brothers of Maria Gomez before tackling Harold Cartwright. He went over to Doctor Mayberry's clinic first to inquire about Miles Townsend's condition. The deputy sheriff was sitting up in bed, being fed a bowl of soup by the doctor's wife. Townsend was still ashen from the loss of blood, but he seemed on the mend already.

"The Gomez brothers own the *cantina,*" Townsend told Amos, giving the lawman directions. "It ain't really nothing but an old adobe shack with a few cribs out back for the whores they have. Antonio . . . he's the oldest of the two, is a mean-talking greaser, but don't let that fool you, Wicklund. He's a coward and a drunk, to boot. The younger one, Juan, is the most dangerous of the two. He carries a damned pig-sticker in his boot and he ain't afraid to use it."

"Do they savvy English?" Amos asked.

"Yeh, but they play like they don't understand a word," Townsend smiled. "If they try to give you that shit you just rap the fuckers a good one and they'll talk your language. But remember what I said about Juan . . . he ain't especially partial to the law asking questions."

"How come a mean fucker like Juan didn't try to get back at Billy Cavenaugh for killing the sister?" Amos asked. "You know how much family honor means to the Mexicans."

"You don't know the Gomez brothers," Townsend scoffed. "The only thing that pissed them off was when Maria went to work for the banker and his wife instead of letting them turn her into one of their whores. I expected trouble from them right off when Billy first started making up to Maria, so I warned Juan and Antonio to mind their own business. Both of them said they didn't give a fuck what she did. After Billy killed the girl I had another talk with them, *pronto*. They didn't seem to give a shit that she was dead. Juan just shrugged and said 'good riddance to the slut.' "

"I'll have a talk with them anyway. Do you need anything, Miles?"

Assured that the deputy sheriff needed nothing, Amos Wicklund left and made his way to the squalid Mexican ghetto on the edge of town. Amos had spent almost his whole life in the southwest, and he held no prejudices against the Mexicans, as did most lawmen. To Amos, the only test was a man's respect for the law. Any man who obeyed the law had his respect. Any man who broke the law was Amos' enemy. It was a simple philosophy, but one that worked for him.

Allison's hundred or so Mexicans and half-breeds lived in a cluster of shacks set apart from the rest of town. Their lives were not particularly pleasant, but most managed to eke out an existence through menial jobs. Only two business establishments exclusively served the Mexican ghetto—the *cantina*/whorehouse run by the Gomez brothers, and a tiny store selling food staples and cheap religious objects.

It was *siesta* time when Amos went into the *cantina.* The small building was as squalid inside as out, with a small board bar set atop barrels along one wall, and several roughly-fashioned tables scattered about the room. The room was empty except for a young slattern with greasy black hair and rouged cheeks who sat at one of the tables and filed her nails. Amos guessed that the woman was less than twenty, although she looked twice that age. She looked up at him and smiled, showing her rotting teeth, her eyebrows raised quizzically.

When Amos, speaking in Spanish, asked for the Gomez brothers, the woman shrugged and looked down at her nails again. Amos repeated the question, more insistently this time. The whore shrugged again and made a gesture with her thumb toward the curtained doorway along the back wall. Amos could feel the woman's eyes examining him as he moved past her and through the door and into the bright sun at the back of the *cantina.* There were five tiny buildings scattered about, two of which Amos recognized as latrines from their foul stench. The three larger shacks were cribs for the use of the whores and their customers. Amos found a naked whore sprawled on the cot in the nearest crib. The woman's fat flesh was none too clean and her legs were covered with insect bites. A crucifix hung above the cot just above the snoring woman's face.

Moving on to the next crib, Amos saw that it was empty. He turned toward the third, hearing noises from that direction. The animal-like grunts and obscene sounds became louder as he neared the shack. The crib's door hung open and Amos peered into the darkness, surprised to see the sweating figure of a man in obvious pleasure sitting on the edge of the bed. A thin young girl knelt on the floor in front of him, her painted mouth sliding up and down over the stub of hardened flesh at the man's loins. Neither had seen Amos yet. He stood there a moment, disgusted by the sight and sounds coming from the two, deciding whether or not to interrupt this crude passion. The man on the bed was in his twenties, Amos guessed. He was overweight, with swarthy features, a thick mustache, and long black hair matted now by the heat and his obscene movements.

Suddenly the girl caught sight of Amos out of the corner of her eye and pulled her mouth away from the man's penis, crying out in alarm. Jesus, Amos thought bitterly, she can't be a day over twelve! The man's eyes flew open and he snarled something unintelligible in Spanish when he saw Amos outside.

"Señor Gomez?" Amos inquired casually.

"Si, *Antonio* Gomez," the man replied, noticing Amos' badge for the first time. The girl had tried to crawl away, but Gomez grabbed her brutally by her naked shoulder, ordering her to stay where she was. "Come back later . . . I busy now," he said to Amos.

"Your pleasure can wait," Amos replied, shaking his head. "Send the girl away. I need to ask you some questions . . . questions about your sister Maria."

"I have no sister!" Gomez growled, waving his arm at Amos. "Go away! I no answer no damned questions!"

The stench inside the crib was almost as bad as that which had come from the latrines, but Amos forced himself to move inside. The room was less than eight feet square, barely large enough for the cot, a small table, and a leather trunk. The young whore watched in wide-eyed horror as Amos grabbed Gomez's hand and jerked it from her shoulder. "Go on, git!" he ordered the girl, moving back so she could scurry by him. She did not bother to cover her naked body as she fled.

When Amos turned back toward the bed he saw Gomez reaching under the dirty pillow. His own gun came out of the worn leather holster before the man could reach the revolver under the pillow. "Drop it or you're a dead man," Amos warned. He waited until Gomez sat upright again before holstering his gun.

"Come on," he ordered, disgusted by the foul odor of the shack. "Get your pants on and we'll go find some fresh air so we can have our little talk."

Amy Cartwright watched from the front window as her husband got into his buggy and went back to the bank after lunch. It had been a silent and cheerless meal, with Harold ignoring his wife as he wolfed down his food. She could see that he was preoccupied—no, *worried* was a better word, she thought. When she asked if there was something wrong, the banker only shook his head sullenly and told her to mind her own business. Hurt, Amy did not attempt further conversation, except to tell Harold that she would be coming into Allison to do some shopping later in the afternoon.

"No!" he had barked. "I don't want you in town. If you need anything, give me a list and I'll bring it out tonight."

"But, why?"

"Never mind why, you just do as I tell you!" Harold had said cryptically.

As soon as her husband's buggy was out of sight, Amy went upstairs, puzzled and angry by Harold's irrational behavior. First, he had refused to hire anyone to take Maria's place, then the increasing jealousy—followed by the brutal way he had taken her the afternoon before. Now this. Was he going to keep her a prisoner? she wondered. She was his wife, she told herself, not some servant to be ordered around.

Amy went into the bathroom and turned on the taps in the tub. It was stifling in the house and she wanted to get into the cool water and let it wash away the hurt she felt. Harold had argued against the cost of installing the expensive tiled bathroom and gravity-feed water system, but Amy had been adamant—"she might have to live in the wilderness," she had told him, "but she wasn't going to do without *every* necessity." Despite his love of ostentatious living, Harold Cartwright hated spending money for what he considered unnecessary luxury, especially when it came to Amy's comfort.

She undressed slowly, looking at her body in the full-length mirror, grimacing when she saw the discoloration along her thighs and breasts from her husband's cruel hands. She almost hated the sight of her naked flesh and the way it inspired such sickening lust in her husband and other men. Why couldn't she be plain and unattractive so that Harold would leave her alone? she wondered bitterly. She got into the tub and lay down, shivering from the unexpected coolness. Then, taking a piece of soft flannel, she let her gentle hands begin to massage away the painful bruises Harold had inflicted. She shivered, feeling her nipples suddenly rise to an unwanted erectness from the tender touch of her fingers. Involuntarily she was taken back to the times when, as a young girl, she had explored her own body this way. It had been exciting and wicked, letting her fingers slide over the unripened breasts, then down along her flat stomach and into the hairless crevice between her thighs. That had always been the most exciting part, that momentary pause before her fingers slithered into the immature flesh of her vagina, sending tingles of mysterious delight racing through her confused mind and body.

Lost in thought, Amy was barely aware she was reenacting one of those remembered moments. To her mind it was only a welcome relief from the brutality her husband had inflicted the afternoon before but, to her hands, it was an unspoken command. Without really being aware of what she was doing, her fingers were guiding the soft cloth over her belly and her trembling thighs were opening slightly to admit the cloth's smoothness up into her furry slit. She gasped as one finger touched the bud of her clitoris hidden in the soft folds of creamy flesh, and she blushed furiously, snapping back into reality. The fantasy had been so wonderful, so exciting, she thought, reddening with shame. If only Harold could be gentle and tender when he made love to her, instead of pawing at her naked flesh and hurting her in his awkward rush to find his own pleasure. But, no, he didn't care what she wanted or needed. And, as a consequence, he had never been able to arouse his wife's dormant sexuality.

Still blushing, she got up from the tub and dried herself, then put on fresh clothing and went downstairs again. She sat down at her writing deak and took up her pen. It would not be an easy thing for her to admit defeat and ask her parents to allow her to return home. But Harold's latest brutality had been the final straw. Amy knew their marriage was hopeless. She just couldn't continue to live with a man who treated her no better than a whore, surrounded by uncivilized people with whom she had nothing in common. Her parents would be upset, she knew, but they would stand by her and help.

The letter was only half-finished when she was suddenly interrupted by a knock at the front door. Amy got up and went to the window, peeking out through the lace curtains, surprised to see a tall, lean man standing on the porch. The man was dressed in faded jeans, a dark shirt, and leather vest, and he was holding a worn Stetson in one hand. His other hand was wrapped in a bandage. For a moment, Amy was tempted to pretend there was no one home. She had never seen this man before and her paranoia over Maria's death was still very much alive in the young wife. Then, telling herself she was being foolish, Amy went to the door and put on the heavy chain before opening it a crack and peering out at the man.

"Yes? What do you want?"

"Afternoon, m'am," Tom Cavenaugh said. "Would you be Mrs. Cartwright?"

For the first time she noticed the scar creasing his forehead. She shivered, wondering who the man was. He seemed polite and pleasant enough, but the scar and the hard, unemotional eyes frightened her.

"Yes, I'm Mrs. Cartwright," she replied hesitantly, "what business do you have with me?"

"It's about the girl who was killed, Mrs. Cartwright," Tom said slowly, "I'd like . . ."

Before he could go on, Amy started to slam the door shut.

"Please, m'am, can't you spare me a moment?" Tom pleaded. "It's very important!"

His voice sounded so urgent that Amy hesitated.

Tom could see the beautiful woman was terrified, an emotion that was perfectly understandable under the circumstances. Still, he had a job to do, and that job was more important than anything else.

"Please, hear me out, m'am," he went on softly, not wanting to alarm the women further. "The fact is, I'm the brother of the man they think killed your servant girl. I don't mean you any harm, nor do I want to frighten you. All I want to do is ask a few questions and have a look at the girl's quarters out back."

The words only served to frighten her even more. Suddenly, Tom Cavenaugh smiled disarmingly.

"I'm sorry, m'am," he said. "It's obvious that I've upset you. I'd better take up the matter with your husband. Please accept my apologies for disturbing you."

He moved away from the door as it slammed behind him.

Still alarmed, Amy hurried to the window and peered out again, half-afraid that the man was somehow going to trick her by pretending to leave and then coming back. She watched him put on his hat and start toward town. Suddenly she remembered something she had heard about Billy Cavenaugh's brother—that he was a U.S. marshal. If that was so, there seemed no reason to fear him. Besides, she told herself, she couldn't spend the rest of her life in terror of every male stranger she met. Impulsively, she ran to the door and threw it open, calling out to him.

"Wait, please," she said, coming out onto the porch.

Tom stopped, then turned and came back toward the house, a puzzled expression on his face. And, for the first time, he was aware of what a truly beautiful woman Amy Cartwright was. She stood there waiting for him, her tall body exciting under the dark silk dress she wore, the low-cut bodice exposing a wide expanse of smooth flesh, the tight cut at the waist pushing her breasts up provocatively. She was not smiling, but her lovely features were soft and fresh. And, even though her honey-colored hair was pulled back and tied in a bun, Tom found it easy to imagine how she would look with the curls hanging loose and easy over her shoulders.

Amy could feel his eyes examining her but, strangely, she wasn't offended as she usually was when men leered at her. For one thing, she told herself, blushing inwardly, this man's gaze was one of frank appreciation for a beautiful woman—not simply the obscene and disgusting way other men undressed her with their eyes.

"I didn't mean to be rude," Amy explained quickly when Tom came back up onto the porch. "It's just that I've been so upset over Maria's death. Then, to have a stranger come asking questions so unexpectedly . . ."

She left the sentence unfinished, obviously distressed.

"I understand, Mrs. Cartwright," Tom replied, nodding. He had taken off his hat again and was fingering the brim while he spoke. "I don't expect you to take my word for it, m'am, but my brother didn't kill the girl. He loved her and wanted to marry Maria and take her to California so they could start a life out there."

"But . . . all the evidence . . . them finding him in bed with her! I know how you must feel losing your brother, Mr. Cavenaugh, but . . ."

She shrugged, not knowing what to say. The pain was clear in Tom Cavenaugh's eyes, she could see, and anger, as well. It had been a terrible thing, the lynching of Billy Cavenaugh—sending him to his death without even a trial!

"I understand you weren't here the night it happened," Tom said. When Amy nodded, Tom went on. "Did Maria Gomez ever hint that my brother had mistreated her in any way?"

"No, but we weren't at all close . . . she was a servant, not a friend. And I didn't even know she was friendly with your brother until he came out here one night and my husband had to run him off. Believe me, Mr. Cavenaugh, there's nothing I can tell you that would help."

"Was she a promiscuous girl?" Tom asked, hoping his frankness wouldn't be misunderstood. "What I mean is, were there other men who she liked? I've heard she was something of a tease."

"I have no knowledge of how Maria behaved when she was out of my sight," Amy replied, rather hotly. That was a lie, of course, Amy realized. Maria had flirted with every man with whom she came into contact. But she could hardly tell this stranger that her own husband was one of those men. "As far as I was concerned, she did her work well enough and gave me no trouble. While Maria was in my employ I found no reason to be dissatisfied with her behavior. I'm afraid that's all I can tell you. I'm sorry."

Tom was disappointed. He had expected Amy Cartwright to know more about her young servant. It seemed strange that two women could be together for several months—even as mistress and servant—and not come to know one another rather well.

Tom sighed, then went on.

"Would you have any objection to my looking at the girl's quarters?" he asked. "I understand she had a place of her own out back."

"My husband *insisted* on that arrangement, Mr. Cavenaugh," Amy replied. "There was adequate room in the house for Maria, but Harold seemed to feel it was somehow inappropriate to have a Mexican sleeping under the same roof as himself." She paused, smiling wryly. "I'm afraid my husband is something of a bigot when it comes to Mexicans and Indians. At any rate, when they were building the house, some of the workmen threw up a small building out back for their tools. Harold had it cleaned up and put in a few sticks of furniture for Maria. She seemed to prefer the arrangement."

"Can I see it?"

"It's gone," Amy replied. Seeing the confusion in Tom's eyes, she added, "What I mean is, my husband had the building torn down after Maria's death. One of the girl's brothers came out one day to collect her things . . . a thoroughly disreputable-looking man named Juan, I think. Harold asked him if he'd tear down the building and told him he could keep any lumber he salvaged for his trouble."

Tom cursed silently. It seemed a strange thing for Cartwright to have done. Still, perhaps the banker had only been thinking of his wife's sensibilities: It couldn't be pleasant living within sight of the murder scene. It was odd, but did not necessarily arouse suspicion. There seemed to be little more he could gain from questioning the lovely young wife. At the same time, he was reluctant to leave. Amy Cartwright was a beautiful and cultured woman—a rarity in Arizona, and Tom hesitated to say good-bye, knowing he would probably never see her again.

Suddenly there was the sound of a horse and buggy on the road from town. Tom looked over his shoulder to see it stop in front of the house and a large man dressed in a dark suit and white silk shirt climbing down. There was a scowl on the man's sleek face as he hurried up the walk.

"What in the hell are you doing out here, Cavenaugh?" the man roared.

Tom had little doubt that the man was Harold Cartwright from the gasp of surprise and distress coming from the young woman on the porch.

"Have we met?" Tom asked calmly.

"No, but I know who you are," Harold Cartwright roared. "And, by God, I don't ever want to see your face around here again." He looked up toward his wife. "What's going on, Amy? What have you and this bastard been talking about behind my back?"

"Harold, please!" she protested, embarrassed by the irrational outburst. "Mr. Cavenaugh simply asked me a few questions about Maria. Why are you so upset?"

"Don't you know who he *is*?" Cartwright asked loudly. "This is the brother of the man who raped and murdered Maria! And here you are entertaining him as if he was the goddamned governor of the territory!"

The banker was red-faced and sweating with fury as he spoke. Tom could see the man's words were having a terrible effect on Amy Cartwright. She reacted as if he had struck her across the face. She tried to say something in her own defense, but the banker waved aside her protest, turning to Tom again.

"I want you off my property right now, damn it! Haven't you and that murdering brother of yours caused us enough grief? You may have Miles Townsend fooled, mister, but I know your kind! And, by God, you'll pay for those killings last night. I'm not without influence in Arizona, as you'll soon find out. Now go on and get off my property before I get my shotgun and run you off like I did that bastard brother of yours! And you leave my wife alone, understand?"

Tom's blood was boiling from the insulting words, but he forced himself to remain cool, although it was a monumental task.

"I'll leave, Mr. Cartwright," he said through clenched teeth, adding, "but you'll eat those words, mister, count on that." He looked up at Amy Cartwright and forced a smile. The woman was near tears from her outrage and anguish. "I'll say good afternoon, m'am. Please accept my apologies for disturbing you."

Cartwright brushed past Tom and up onto the porch. "Damn you, Amy, get inside," he screamed. When the woman didn't move as quickly as the banker had wished, he grabbed her arm roughly and shoved her through the doorway, causing his wife to cry out in real pain. "Go on, get moving!"

There was no hesitation in Tom as he took the porch steps at one leap. Cartwright was preparing to follow his wife into the house, one hand upraised as if he were going to hit his wife. Tom grabbed him by the shoulder and spun him around.

"Mister, I don't care how much influence you have, you'll not mistreat a woman in my presence," he warned, shaking his balled fist under the banker's face. Cartwright's eyes widened in shock and he tried to pull away.

"Don't touch me, Cavenaugh," he shrieked. "You can't tell me how to treat my own wife!"

Amy Cartwright was standing in the doorway and she pleaded with Tom. "No, don't . . . he didn't hurt me," she begged, afraid that Tom Cavenaugh was about to kill her husband.

Tom ignored the woman, concentrating his attention on the banker. "I am telling you, mister," he went on, trembling with rage. "Wife or not, don't you ever lay another hand on this lady or you'll have me to deal with. I've taken your insults when I should have put a bullet through you, but you're pressing your luck when you start mistreating females!"

Cartwright was still gasping in fright when Tom turned and went back down the steps and then out into the road. When he was off the banker's property, Tom turned and looked back. The banker had disappeared into the house but he caught a glimpse of Amy Cartwright's ashen face as she shut the door. Tom smiled and gave a salute with his hand, then walked slowly back into town, half-expecting the banker to come after him with his shotgun.

No, Tom told himself, that isn't the Cartwright's style. The man was a coward, one who would feel more at ease mistreating helpless women than in facing down a man. Tom suddenly wondered if Maria Gomez had been subjected to Harold Cartwright's insane rages and physical violence?

There was one hell of a lot more he wanted to know about the banker and his friends, Tom told himself. Especially the missing Jeb Fallon and Marcus Owens, the two who had spent that fateful evening with the banker while Maria Gomez was being murdered a short distance away.

As he went into the Allison jail, Tom wondered how Amos Wicklund had fared with Harold Cartwright and the Gomez brothers. The door to the jail was open, but Amos was nowhere in sight. "Amos?" he called out, striding over to the doorway that separated the jail office from the cells at the rear.

"Amos?" he called out again when there was no answer.

Suddenly he was alert as he saw that the cell doors were open, that Carl Conroy and Will Hoffstader were gone. Cursing, he raced back into the office, checking the worn desk to see if Amos Wicklund had left any message for him.

There was none.

Chapter Five

Two young boys playing in a dry wash at the northern end of town found Amos Wicklund's body late that afternoon. The marshal lay on his stomach, his limbs twisted, his holster empty, flies already buzzing around his corpse.

Tom was at Doctor Mayberry's clinic with Miles Townsend when the parents of one of the boys arrived with the news. "I think it's that U. S. marshal," the man said nervously. "I saw him in town this morning. I can't be sure, of course, but it sure looks like him."

"Show me!" Tom demanded, bolting for the door with the man in close pursuit. The doctor grabbed up his medical bag and followed after ordering the agitated Miles Townsend to remain in bed.

The news had already spread by the time Tom and the doctor arrived at the wash, and a crowd of men and boys stood at the scene looking down at the body. Pushing them aside, Tom did not have to turn the corpse over to recognize that it was his old friend. Doctor Mayberry knelt beside him, putting on his glasses before he leaned closer to examine the lifeless flesh.

"A stab wound," he murmured, pulling Amos' vest up and peering at the ripped, bloody shirt and small wound beneath. Watching, Tom wondered at how such a tiny wound could snuff out his friend's life. It was no more than two inches long, but the blade had been expertly jammed home between the ribs, probably piercing his friend's heart. The doctor confirmed Tom's guess. "I'd say he died instantly," he said, turning to say something to one of the men in the crowd. "Basil, go fetch the undertaker, will you?"

Tom stood up, facing the crowd, his face hard and not betraying the grief and pain he felt. "Is there anyone here who knows anything about this?" he asked, looking around at the faces. No one answered, but many shook their heads. "Did anyone see Marshal Wicklund this afternoon?" Tom went on. "Damn it, answer me!"

A bearded man pushed his way to the front of the crowd. "I saw him leave the jail about two o'clock," he said. "He was heading out toward greaser town."

"Did anybody else see him?"

Two more men confirmed that Amos had, indeed, been seen walking toward the Mexican section of Allison, but they disagreed on the time. One man said it was closer to three o'clock, the other man thought it was about one-thirty.

"All right, the three of you go back to the jail and wait for me," Tom ordered. "The rest of you go home . . . there's nothing here to see." When the crowd hesitated, Tom's voice rose. "Go on, get the fuck out of here, the lot of you!"

When they were gone, Tom knelt down beside the body again and helped the doctor turn Amos over. The lawman's lifeless eyes were open and staring up, a surprised expression on the dead face. Somehow Amos looked much older than he had in life. Taking off his shirt, Tom covered his friend's face, brushing away the flies at the same time.

Tom already knew that Amos had been to the clinic to see Miles Townsend around two o'clock, that he had left shortly thereafter to find the Gomez brothers. He listened quietly as the doctor told him his friend had been dead three hours at most.

"Will you wait for the undertaker and see he gets back to town?" Tom asked, standing up and looking at the doctor. The doctor nodded, asking where Tom was going. "To find the Gomez brothers," Tom answered coldly.

"Then you'd better take some men with you," the doctor sighed, wondering how many more corpses he would be called on to examine before the day was out. "If Antonio or Juan did this to your friend they're not just going to stand around and let you arrest them."

Tom was already gone before the sentence was finished.

Ten minutes later he burst into the *cantina*, ignoring the crowd of children which had begun to follow him as soon as he reached the Mexican settlement. The small *cantina* was packed with badly-dressed Mexicans drinking and listening to an old man who strummed a guitar in the corner. Three females, obviously whores from their appearance and dress, danced in front of the musician, shaking their bodies lewdly while they shouted obscenties at those watching. The oppressive heat and the sickening odors that contrasted with the cool air outside staggered Tom for a moment.

Suddenly the music and the voices died off as someone saw Tom and yelled to the crowd. Every face in the room turned to look at him.

"Where are the Gomez brothers?" Tom shouted.

When no one answered, he grabbed the nearest man and yanked him to his feet. He was a young Mexican with pock-marked, dark skin and bad teeth. Speaking in Spanish this time, Tom repeated the question.

"Gone," the sullen man answered. He smiled sarcastically when someone laughed. *"Gone,* señor!"

The smile left his face when he felt the cold steel of Tom's gun pressing against his temple. "Gone *where*?" Tom demanded, cocking the hammer. Suddenly there were screams as the three whores fell to the floor and crawled under one of the tables in terror.

A fat, middle-aged man yelled something to Tom from behind the crude bar where he stood. Still holding the gun barrel against the younger man's head, Tom turned toward the voice, his eyebrows raised quizzically.

"The brothers Gomez left an hour ago, señor," the fat man said laconically. "I bought this place from them, *comprende*?"

"Where are they headed?"

The man shrugged his fat shoulders.

"Who knows? Tucson, perhaps . . . maybe Nogales. What you want with them?"

"If you're lying to me I'll come back and kill you!" Tom warned, meaning every word of what he said. "Is what you told me true?"

Suddenly several people were swearing to the barman's story, including the man with the gun to his head. "It's true, señor," he said hoarsely. "Some *gringo* come arrest them today . . . took them to jail. An hour later Antonio and Juan come back . . . say *gringo* lawman tell them to leave Allison *pronto*! They sell *cantina* to Julio and go quick! I swear this on the grave of my mother, señor!"

If Amos had arrested the Gomez brothers it seemed unlikely that he had gotten them back to the jail without being seen by anyone in town. More likely, one of the Mexicans had managed to kill Amos and then dump his body in the dry wash. Despite their pleas to be believed, Tom had no illusions that the Mexicans were telling the truth about where the Gomez brothers had gone, or when they left. He stared at the man to whose head his gun was pressed. "You're lying, you bastard," he snarled.

Thinking he was about to be killed, the man screamed for mercy. "No! I swear it! Don't shoot me, señor!"

Tom knew he was wasting time. Repeating his warning, he holstered his gun and pushed his way out of the *cantina*, retracing his steps into town. He went directly to the livery stable and ordered the man there to saddle his horse, telling him to bring the horse around to the doctor's clinic as quickly as possible. When he reached the doctor's surgery, Miles Townsend was already up and dressed, despite the doctor's frantic pleas for him to remain in bed.

Tom told the lawman what he had discovered, informing Townsend that he was going after Juan and Antonio Gomez. "At least wait long enough for me to get up a posse," Townsend protested.

"Take your posse and round up Carl Conroy and Will Hoffstader," Tom replied impatiently. "If you don't hear from me by this time tomorrow, get word to Prescott and tell them what's happened."

Townsend was in obvious pain from his shoulder wound, but he quickly agreed to do as Tom asked. He watched as Tom went outside and climbed onto his waiting horse. Then, waving aside the continuing objections of Doctor Mayberry, Miles Townsend strapped on his gun and went to raise the posse.

The road south led from Allison to Pine Mesa, the same trail Tom had ridden the day before. He guessed that if the Gomez brothers had, indeed, headed for Tucson or Nogales, they they would take the main road rather than one of the slower mountain trails. It was only supposition on his part, but he assumed they would want to put distance between themselves and Allison as quickly as possible.

Tom pushed his horse hard, grateful for the bright moon which allowed him good visibility through the heavily-forested first few miles. As he rode he thought about Amos Wicklund. With Amos' death, two of the men most important in Tom's life were now gone. It was almost as if fate had placed him under some sort of curse, punishing him for an inexplicable reason. Why had the Gomez brothers murdered Amos? What had the lawman discovered about them that necessitated his killing. Amos' death had added new grief to old, filling Tom with rage at those who had committed the cowardly acts of lynching and murder.

His mind was filled with hatred. He wanted to lash out at the whole damned world for what had happened to Billy and Amos Wicklund. There was no doubt in his mind that the two killings were connected somehow. Someone wanted Billy out of the way before he could stand trial. But why? And why had Tom's arrival in Allison raised such fears in the minds of Harold Cartwright, Jeb Fallon, and Marcus Owens? What was it about Maria Gomez's death that triggered paranoia in the three men?

The forest had thinned out as Tom approached the switchback trail that would carry him down through the canyon to Pine Mesa. That settlement was still miles ahead, but he was making good time, and he prayed that the Gomez brothers would be moving slower. It was darker as he descended into the steep canyon and, with the moon obscured, his horse had to pick its way carefully along the rock-littered trail.

Tom suddenly reined his horse in as he saw a pinpoint of light in the darkness ahead. He guessed the light to be a distance of two to three hundred feet away. Quietly sliding off his horse, Tom tied the animal to the nearest tree, then took his carbine from the scabbard and crept forward. The only sounds came from the wind and the moaning of the huge pines and firs that lined the canyon trail.

As far as Tom knew, there were no settlers living in the canyon, but it was possible that a prospector was working the area. As he got closer to the light he saw that it came from a small campfire in a clearing fifty feet or so off the trail. He could hear voices now, but the words were too softly spoken for him to make out.

Moving forward again, he slipped through the trees so that he could come up from a direction the men around the campfire wouldn't expect. The last fifty feet was slow going. Tom heard the horses before he made out their dark shapes. He counted two animals, their heads down, grazing the lush grass of the clearing.

By now he could hear the voices clearly.

The two men sat facing one another across the fire, their features clearly outlined by the flickering flames. The one nearest Tom was older than his companion and heavier. Both wore loose Mexican peasant shirts over dark trousers, and wide-brimmed felt hats. The older of the two had a rifle lying across his knees and a revolver in a tooled holster on his hip. The other man carried a pistol stuck in his waistband. Both ate as they talked, using a flat rock placed atop the fire to cook their tortillas.

Tom knew from their conversation that he had found the Gomez brothers. Antonio, the eldest of the two, complained in a whining voice that his brother's actions had been those of a crazy man, that they would both be hanged before the month was out. His brother Juan, sneeringly dismissed the complaints, calling Antonio a stupid fool and asking sarcastically if the other hadn't gotten too soft from the whores and the tequila.

"What the hell do you know about whores?" Antonio countered angrily, "*You fucker of little boys*!"

"Shut your stupid month before I do it for you," Juan Gomez laughed mirthlessly. "Are you some kind of saint that you can talk to me like this? At least I never lusted to sleep with my own sister!" He smiled lewdly, baring his teeth. "I wish I had my sweet little Pepe with me now instead of you, you fat-assed pig!"

Tom had heard more than enough. He was less than ten feet from the brothers now. Bringing his rifle up, he aimed it at the head of Juan Gomez. "Don't move a muscle, either of you!" he cried out. "You, Antonio, slide that rifle off your knees!"

Neither man made a sound. Then, slowly, as Tom came forward, Antonio gave a little gasp of fear and started to ease the weapon off his knees. Suddenly he kicked at the fire with his boot heel, rolling to one side as he did. He landed on his side but came up with the rifle in his hands. It exploded, sending a slug past Tom's head. Tom's finger found the trigger of his rifle instinctively. Antonio was behind and to the left of his brother now. Tom's shot caught him square in the chest and sent his body reeling backwards, then crashing to the ground. Antonio died with a dazed expression on his florid face.

Juan Gomez wasted no time when he saw his brother fall. Lean and wiry, he seemed as agile as a cat when he leaped backwards away from the firelight. He pulled the gun from his waist with lightning speed and there were three sharp reports.

The shots splintered the tree to Tom's right. Levering another round into his rifle, Tom fired in the direction from which the shots had come. Juan answered quickly, aiming at the flash from Tom's rifle barrel. But Tom was already several feet away. He tossed the rifle to the ground and laid down a fusillade in Juan's direction with his revolver. He moved as he squeezed off the rounds, never giving Juan a target.

When he stopped to reload he listened intently for any sound from his opponent. The horses were wild with fright and fighting to free themselves from the rope hobbles which kept them from bolting. Knowing that Juan might try to slip away, Tom watched their dark, dancing shapes out of the corner of his eye.

"Give yourself up, Gomez," he called out into the darkness. "You haven't got a chance!"

The answer was a shouted obscenity in Spanish.

All right, you cowardly bastard, Tom thought, *I gave you your chance*!

He was about to fire again when he saw the shadow slipping through the trees toward the horses. Tom waited, swinging the revolver around and aiming at the spot Juan would have to pass in order to get to his horse. It seemed like an eternity before he saw the dark shape pass between the two trees and dash for his animal.

Juan was crouching low as he ran, presenting a difficult target. Now! Tom's mind shouted silently. His finger contracted and he felt the revolver buck, then heard the scream of pain over the snorting of the horses. Juan seemed to hang in the air forever, his body twisting madly as he fought to return the fire. Tom fired again, grunting with satisfaction when he saw the shadow fall to the ground.

He was too wise to go directly toward the fallen man. Instead, he made his way out to the rocky trail and then around behind Juan, working his way through the trees without sound. His caution was justified, he saw, when he neared Juan and saw that, despite his wounds, the Mexican was stifling his moans and waiting for him from the other direction, his gun cocked and ready.

It would have been easy for Tom to put a bullet in the man's head and end it all. Instead, Tom slipped silently up behind the Mexican and thrust his gun against Juan's head.

"Drop it!" he ordered.

Juan's gun fell from his trembling hand and he swung around, screaming curses and obscenities at Tom between his moans of pain. Tom picked up the other man's pistol and tossed it as far as he could. Then, still holding his gun to Juan's head, he ordered his prisoner to crawl over to the campfire. It was hard going for the wounded man, but he finally made it. Tom had never seen such hatred on a man's face as the one which stared up at him. Tom's first shot had caught Juan in the fleshy part of his thigh just above the knee. It was not a serious wound, but a painful one. The second one—more serious—had shattered Juan's left elbow, leaving the limb limp and hanging uselessly.

"Why did you kill Amos Wicklund?" Tom demanded.

Gomez grimaced from the agony in his leg and arm. Then, forcing a contemptuous smile, he gathered the saliva in his mouth and spit on his questioner.

"God damn you, Gomez, answer me!" Tom shouted, infuriated by the Mexican's insolence. He stepped back two paces, bringing the barrel of his revolver back and about to swing it at Juan's head to jog the man's memory.

The move almost cost him his life.

Almost before Tom could react the Mexican slid his right hand down to his elaborately tooled boots. The knife hidden there seemed to jump into his slender fingers, the cold hard steel glimmering in the flickering firelight. The blade flashed upward as Juan came up on his good leg.

Tom watched in shock, expecting at any second to feel the murderous steel sliding through his shirt and into the flesh and muscles of his stomach. Only at the last minute did he manage to suck in his stomach and give himself enough time to swing his gun barrel down. The vicious blow laid open Juan's head, splitting the flesh like a ripe melon. Blood gushed out to cover Tom's revolver and fingers. At the same time as he swung the gun barrel, Tom brought his boot up and kicked the Mexican as hard as he could in the groin. There was a shrill shriek of pain and Juan's eyes widened in disbelief. His agony was so intense that his fingers involuntarily relaxed around the knife blade, letting it fall to the ground. He started to say something but no words came out, only a gutteral and incoherent cry. Then, while Tom watched, the man's lean body collapsed.

Breathing hard from his close call, Tom stood there for several moments before moving to pick up the knife and jab the blade deeply into the nearest tree. He held the handle for a second and then gave a vicious twist, breaking the razor-sharp blade in half.

He was exhausted, but he knew his efforts were far from over. His first priority was in finding medical attention for Juan Gomez before the man bled to death from his wounds. Antonio was beyond help now, his lifeless body already growing cold in the night air. As far as Tom knew, there was no doctor in the small settlement of Pine Mesa. That meant transporting Juan back to Allison, a distance of nearly ten miles.

Working quickly, Tom bound up the unconscious man's wounds as best he could. Juan moaned piteously as Tom worked. When he finally did come around, Juan was in too much pain to give Tom any further trouble. It was an effort to lift the dead man and his brother to their horses and tie them on, but Tom finally managed.

Retrieving his own horse, they started back up the trail toward Allison.

Deputy Sheriff Miles Townsend was having his own troubles.

He had been able to round up and deputize only eight men for his posse. Others, knowing what a powerful man Jim Conroy was in that part of Arizona, wanted no part of the hunt for Carl Conroy and Will Hoffstader. They declined Townsend's invitation to join the posse, pleading a variety of excuses as to why they could not fulfill their civic responsibility. Disgusted and angry at their response, he decided to make do with the few men he did have.

When and how Carl Conroy and Hoffstader had gotten out of jail was still a mystery to the sheriff. He had found no sign of any *forced* break-out—the keys to the cells were still on the peg in the jail office—and he could find no one who had seen or heard anything. The only theory that made any sense was that someone from the Conroy Ranch had slipped into the jail while Amos Wicklund was searching for the Gomez brothers. And, if that were so, it meant that the two prisoners were probably back at the ranch now. And that meant trouble. Jim Conroy had at least a dozen hands working the ranch besides J. R. Gilman and the other man who had been killed in the whorehouse. Gilman had been the meanest, of course, but the others were almost as bad. If Carl and Will Hoffstader had gone back to the ranch, it would be no easy feat to take them again.

The ranch itself covered several thousand acres at the head of Sweetwater Valley, a combination of forest, mountains, and prime grazing land on which Jim Conroy ran his herd of beef. The main ranchhouse, the bunkhouse, and the various other out-buildings lay a mile or so off the road to Ash Fork, which ran through the Conroy property, and was in an area easy to defend. If Townsend was right about the escapees being there, he told himself, they would be expecting trouble and prepared for him and his posse.

"All right, boys, let's go," he told his men. "I want Carl and Will Hoffstader alive, if possible, but I aim to bring them back to Allison either way. You've all been deputized temporarily, so if anything happens to me, see that the law is carried out. Any questions?"

When there were none, Townsend spurred his horse forward, followed by the others. They rode as hard and as fast as the sheriff's wounds would allow. Miles could feel his wound reopen under the bandages, and the warm blood staining his shirt. The pain of being in the saddle again so soon was awful. He prayed that he was physically up to what he had to do.

If not, he might find his own body joining the increasing number of corpses building up in the small shed behind Allison's undertaker's parlor.

* * *

Tom rode back into Allison about an hour after Townsend and the posse had left for the Conroy Ranch. The streets were quiet and deserted, and he went directly to the jail. A curious drunk stopped in the street when he saw Tom pulling Juan Gomez off the horse. Tom ordered the man to help him get Gomez into the jail and then to go and fetch Doctor Mayberry. They took the wounded man directly into the cell which had so recently held Carl Conroy, putting him on the hard metal cot. Tom could see that Juan was in bad shape, but he shackled the Mexican's feet to the end of the bunk nonetheless.

In a few moments the doctor came in. The physician shook his head in amazement at the carnage wrought on Juan Gomez, then quickly went to work on his new patient. As he treated the wounds, Mayberry told Tom about Townsend riding out to the Conroy Ranch in search of the two escaped prisoners.

"He could only raise eight men, though," Mayberry said in disgust. "I'm beginning to think ninety percent of the men in this town are cowards!"

"What kind of shape was Miles in?" Tom asked, concerned for the sheriff.

"He'll be lucky if he makes it out there at all," Mayberry replied cynically. "By the way, is that Antonio Gomez's body tied to the horse outside?"

Tom told the doctor what had happened when he caught up with the brothers and tried to bring them in. "You're going to make a rich man out of the undertaker," Mayberry said. He stood up, looking grim. "I don't know if this one will live or not," he went on. "The leg wound isn't serious, but the arm will have to be amputated. I don't know, he's lost a hell of a lot of blood to chance that kind of surgery now. I think I'll wait until morning and see how he is before deciding."

The doctor reached into his bag and took out a syringe, filling the instrument with liquid from a small bottle. "Wait a minute," Tom protested. "What's that you're giving him?"

"Something to make him sleep so he doesn't jump around and lose more blood," Mayberry answered.

"But, damn it, I need to question him."

Mayberry paused, holding the syringe in his hand.

"Son, this man is going to be dead in an hour if he starts bleeding again. Is that what you want?"

It wasn't, but neither did Tom want the Mexican's death on his conscience, even though Juan had been ready enough to use his knife and his gun on Tom, and had no doubt murdered Amos Wicklund.

"All right, do what you have to," he said in frustrated resignation. "I'm going out to the Conroy ranch if you'll give me directions. Will you take care of this scum until I get back? And do something with Antonio's body?"

Assured that Mayberry would handle those things, Tom took his tired mount over to the stable and exchanged the weary horse for a fresh animal. In a few minutes he was back in the saddle and on his way to join Miles Townsend and the small posse.

The lights were on in the front parlor of the Cartwright House as Tom's horse galloped past. Harold Cartwright looked up from his brandy at the sound of the horse and rider, then over at Marcus Owens.

Owens was clearly a thoroughly frightened man. The heavy-set owner of the general store sweated profusely as he wrung his fat fingers nervously. "Damn it, Harold, you've got to do something!" he cried out for the third time in as many minutes. "This whole goddamned thing is falling apart! You swore you'd handle things . . . see that nothing got out of hand!"

"And I *will,* Marcus," the banker assured his friend.

"Oh, yeh, you're doing a *beautiful* job of it!" Owens said sarcastically. "People being killed all over the place . . . that fucker Fallon running off like a scared rabbit, now those two assholes killing a goddamned U. S. marshal! Oh, you're taking care of things all right! Jesus, how did we ever get mixed up in this thing?"

Harold Cartwright could see that Marcus Owens was very near falling apart completely. The thought of that happening frightened the banker very much. And it almost sickened him to watch the blubbery-faced Owens acting like some panic-stricken female instead of a man.

"You know very well how you got mixed up in this *thing*, as you call it," Cartwright said hotly, nearing the end of his patience. "Whose idea was it in the first place? Mine? Oh, no, my friend, you're not putting all the blame on me! You and Jeb were the ones who wanted to . . ."

The banker suddenly stopped, an expression of alarm on his face as he looked over toward the sliding doors which closed off the parlor from the rest of the house. Putting his finger to his lips, he arose from his chair and went quickly to the doors, grasping the handle of one and jerking it. The door slid into its wall recess.

Amy Cartwright stood there, a confused, frightened expression on her drawn face. She gasped at the sight of her husband, blushing furiously.

"What are you doing out here eavesdropping on us?" Cartwright cried out angrily.

"Nothing . . . honestly," Amy replied nervously backing away toward the stairway which led upstairs. "I heard someone come in and and I . . . I . . ."

"Don't you lie to me, damn it!" her husband snarled. "I told you to stay upstairs tonight, didn't I? Well, then, what are you doing down here snooping?"

The angry accusations only served to increase Amy's distress. She had gone up to her room directly after dinner when Harold had said he was having someone in and didn't want to be disturbed. Unable to sleep, she had come downstairs for a glass of warm milk.

Hearing the angry voices in the parlor, she had naturally been curious. She tried to explain all that to her enraged husband, but the banker waved aside her words.

"Get back upstairs," he ordered hoarsely. "We'll discuss this later. Go on!"

Terrified, Amy rushed toward the stairway as her husband glared at her. When she was out of sight, Cartwright came back into the parlor and pulled the door shut again.

"Oh, Jesus, Harold, what if she heard us?" Marcus Owens cried out in panic.

"What if she did!" Cartwright scoffed, feeling less assured than his words indicated. He cursed silently, trying to remember if he and Marcus had said anything which might incriminate them in Amy's mind. He was almost certain that they had not, although the heated discussion had been becoming increasingly frank and dangerous. Facing Marcus Owens again, he smiled. "Don't worry about Amy, Marcus. She's my wife and I'll handle her. Look, I've been thinking . . . perhaps it wouldn't be a bad idea if you got away from Allison yourself until this thing blows over."

"I can't do *that*, Harold," Owens replied, more frightened than before. "Where would I go? Who'd run the store? Besides, it would look like I had something to hide! No, I just can't."

"Do you think you're going to be able to stand up to that bastard Cavenaugh?" Cartwright asked skeptically. "You can't duck him forever, you know. The man's a killer . . . a cold-blooded murderer! He'll get it out of you and then shoot you down like he did Gilman and that other cowboy, Marcus." He paused, seeing the effect his words were having on his overweight friend. Owens was trembling visibly as the banker spoke, and the perspiration poured off his forehead. "But, then, suit yourself, Marcus," Cartwright went on. "Maybe he *won't* kill you. Maybe he'll enjoy the thought of you spending the rest of your life down in the prison at Yuma, more than he would seeing you dead."

Owens was on the verge of hysteria now.

"No! For the love of God, Harold, don't let that happen!" he cried out. "Please, tell me what to do!"

Cartwright hesitated for a moment before going on, gloating over the way he could manipulate Marcus Owens. Everything isn't lost yet, he told himself smugly. And, even if the roof did cave in on their scheme, it wasn't his own ass that was going to be burned. People meant nothing to Harold Cartwright—not Maria Gomez, Marcus Owens and Jeb Fallon, certainly not either of the Cavenaugh brothers. The only thing important to the banker was his own welfare. Even his wife was significant only as a *possession*.

"Tell me what to do, Harold?" Marcus Owens repeated, his voice whining and full of self-pity.

"Well, like I told you before, Marcus, why don't you leave Allison until this whole thing blows over," Cartwright told the other man, trying to make his words sound calm and reassuring. "I'll tell you what, I'll lend you my buggy and a hundred dollars or so. There's no need for you even to tell your wife you're leaving. Write out a note to her and I'll take it in and explain you've got to take care of some business down in Prescott. She won't like it, probably, but I'll make her understand. Look, it's almost midnight. You can wait here until dawn and then get an early start. As soon as things are back to normal you can come back. Go on, now, you can use my desk to write the note to your wife."

Owens seemed almost in a daze as he sat down at the banker's desk and took up the pen and paper Cartwright handed him. The plan seemed so crazy, and his wife would be furious at him running off like this with no believable explanation. Still, he would rather face *her* wrath than that of Tom Cavenaugh. He began to write.

* * *

The pain in Miles Townsend's shoulder was making the lawman dizzy by the time he and the posse reached the Conroy Ranch. They reined in at the front of the main building, surprised that they had encountered none of the ranch hands as yet. There were lights on in the house and in the bunkhouse a few hundred feet away.

"What'll we do, Miles?" one of the men in the posse asked.

"You fellows stay put," he answered, wincing as he climbed down from his horse. "This doesn't look like any kind of trap I ever saw. Maybe Carl and Will didn't come out here after all. Well, we'll soon find out."

Miles walked slowly up onto the long porch that ran the length of the adobe building. Like most ranch-houses this one was built more for utility than esthetics. Long a widower, Jim Conroy had raised his son alone, devoting much less time to the boy than he had to building up the thriving ranch. A crude man, Conroy had surrounded himself with men like J. R. Gilman who spoke his language, men little better than animals.

The deputy sheriff took a deep breath before knocking. The fire in his shoulder was a raging inferno now, and he knew that most of the stitches that Doctor Mayberry had put in were torn loose, allowing the blood to saturate his shirt and vest.

The door was pulled open almost immediately after he rapped.

Townsend was shocked to see the wild-eyed face of old Jim Conroy, the ranch owner, staring back at him. Amos Wicklund had told the deputy about Conroy's angry visit to the jail that morning, and about the ranch owner taking the stage for Prescott.

"I thought you went down to the territorial capital," Miles said, confused.

"That's what I wanted you fuckers to think," Conroy sneered. "You didn't think I was going to leave my boy and Will Hoffstader in that stinking jail of yours, did you?" He paused, seeing the other riders. "What are you doing out here, Townsend?"

"I've come to take Carl and Will back to jail," Miles said simply. "I figured it was you or some of your men that got them out. Where are they?"

There was a mirthless cackle from the older man.

"Oh, they're safe enough," Conroy replied. "But, you ain't taking them nowhere on your goddamned trumped-up charges, deputy! The ones who should be locked up are you and that fucker who shot J. R. and Emil. Carl and my boys was only protecting themselves, as far as I can see. Now you and that pack of assholes with you get off my land, *pronto*!"

"I'll leave when I have Carl and Will with me," Townsend replied as forcefully as his pain would allow. "There's another matter, Conroy, and that concerns you. Your son told us that Harold Cartwright and Jeb Fallon was out here the afternoon they hanged Billy Cavenaugh. As soon as they left, you gave J. R. Gilman money and told him to get the lynch mob stirred up. That kind of coincidence sticks in my craw, Conroy. I want to know why you did it, and if the banker and Fallon put you up to it. Well?"

"That goddamned son of mine and his fucking lies!" the old man cursed. "You want an answer, deputy, well, by Jesus, I'll give you one!"

Conroy's hand disappeared for a moment. When it came back into view, it was holding a doubled-barreled shotgun. Conroy brought the gun up, aiming it at the deputy sheriff.

"You've got one minute to get off my land or I'll blow your damned head off, Townsend!" the rancher warned. "The only way you'll get Carl is over my dead body!"

"If that's what it takes," Townsend nodded, backing away. He almost stumbled coming down off the porch, but he managed to get back to his horse and pull himself into his saddle. The other posse members watched warily, several of them wishing they had turned down the deputy's offer of excitement.

"What now?" one of them asked Miles.

Townsend didn't answer immediately. He watched Conroy come out through the doorway and down off the porch, still holding the shotgun.

"I told you to git!" the old man called out angrily. He looked over his shoulder, toward the house. "Boys! Come out here!"

The porch was suddenly crowded with Conroy's ranch hands, some holding rifles, others with revolvers in their hands. Miles saw that there were at least ten men, and he knew that the hands were ready to fire at him and the posse members on Conroy's command.

"We're leaving, Conroy," Miles called out, "but you haven't heard the last of this. I want Carl and Will Hoffstader returned to the jail by noon tomorrow. If you don't bring them in yourself, you'll be facing every lawman in this part of Arizona." He turned his horse, waving the posse back toward the road with a flick of his hand. "Remember, Conroy . . . *noon tomorrow*!"

If there was any response from the elderly rancher it was lost in the sounds of the posse's horses galloping away. The group slowed when they were out of range of the rancher and his men's weapons.

"He ain't going to bring them in," one of the men said in disgust. "Shit, boys, we just made fools of ourselves coming out here tonight."

"Shut up, McQuaid," Miles told the speaker. "There's a time to fight and a time to back off. We've had enough killings in these past three days." He paused as a wave of nausea swept over him, bringing with it a dizzying tremor. "Somebody help me . . . I don't think I can make it . . ."

The two nearest men moved in quickly to help the swaying deputy. But Miles recovered quickly. Waving them off, he ordered the men back into town. He tried to hide his condition from the men, but he could feel himself slipping back and forth between consciousness and unconsciousness. The man named McQuaid rode beside him, watching for any sign that Townsend was in trouble.

The posse was half-way back to town when they met Tom Cavenaugh. Reining in, they told him what had happened at the Conroy Ranch. Tom cursed when he saw the spreading bloodstain on the deputy's shirt and realized that Townsend was in bad shape. His inclination was to go out to the ranch alone and confront Conroy and his men. That was a fool's game, he told himself. He was too close to the answers now to get himself killed in a senseless shoot-out with a dozen armed and dangerous men.

"All right, let's get back to Allison," he said at last. "We'll figure out how to deal with Conroy after we get the sheriff here back to the doc."

It was well past one o'clock when Tom left the jail and strode over to his hotel. Miles Townsend now lay on an improvised cot in the jail office, with Doctor Mayberry attending him. Most of the possemen had been sent home, but Tom left the most trustworthy-looking of the group to stand guard over Juan Gomez at the jail.

He was bone-weary. It seemed months since he had seen a good night's sleep. Strangely, though, his mind was alert and he wondered if he would be able to get any rest. There were several comfortable chairs on the hotel porch. Tom sat down in one of them and lit a cigar, hoping the smoke would calm him. As he smoked, he tried to put the events of the past few days in some sort of perspective. It was as if he had a gigantic puzzle spread out before him, with all the clues and pieces there for him to see, but without any clear idea how they fit together.

Someone had brutally raped and killed Maria Gomez. According to all the evidence, Billy seemed the logical suspect—a fact that Tom was unwilling to concede. Then, someone—probably Harold Cartwright and Jeb Fallon—had conspired with Jim Conroy to have Billy lynched before he could get a fair trial. That much seemed certain. When he had arrived in Allison and started asking questions, Jeb Fallon had panicked and fled, and the other two men who had found Maria's body refused to answer his questions. The banker had even had Maria's shack torn down. And the dead girl's brothers had murdered Amos Wicklund and then tried to flee when the marshal had started asking questions of them. Perhaps Tom would learn the reason for that killing when he confronted Juan Gomez in the morning. He doubted it. The Mexican would probably refuse to tell him anything, Tom surmised.

His mind kept coming back to the banker and his two friends. Harold Cartwright, Jeb Fallon, and Marcus Owens were the key to the puzzle, of that much he was sure. He guessed that Jim Conroy, J. R. Gilman, Carl Conroy and the other ranch hands, and the Gomez brothers had played secondary roles in the tragedy. They were no less guilty, of course, but he doubted if they had played any part in the young servant-girl's death.

Tom finished his cigar and threw the stub into the street and got up. Tomorrow, he told himself, Harold Cartwright and Marcus Owens were going to answer his questions, and God help either man if the answers were evasive or unsatisfactory. Five men had already died as a result of Maria's death, and Tom was in no mood to let the toll rise without knowing exactly what had happened at the Cartwright house the night of Maria's murder.

He went through the silent hotel lobby and up the stairway to his own room at the far end of the corridor. He had left the door unlocked and it swung open easily. He had just shut the door behind him when he became aware that someone else was in the room. For a moment he was confused, wondering if he had come into the wrong room.

Even before he could open the door again to check the room number, he heard Amy Cartwright's soft voice calling out his name.

"Mr. Cavenaugh," she whispered. "Is that you?"

"Mrs. Cartwright?" Tom asked hoarsely, shocked by the woman's presence. "What are you doing here?"

He started to light the kerosene lamp, but she protested urgently. "No, please, I don't want you to see me like this!"

She sat in the room's only chair, a comfortable rocker near the bed. Tom rushed across the room and knelt beside her. "What's wrong?" he asked, concerned by the tremor in her voice. He could just make out the outline of her body in the darkness. "Did your husband hurt you?"

"It's nothing," she replied, fighting back the tears. "I had a small accident . . . I . . . I fell down the stairs and bruised myself," she lied. "Please, Mr. Cavenaugh, I've got to tell you something."

Tom knew she wasn't telling the truth, but he let it pass for the moment. "Go on," he replied. "What do you want to tell me?"

Amy hesitated, as if fighting the turmoil within herself.

"It's all so horribly mixed-up," she said finally, the hysteria in her voice obvious. "I didn't know who to turn to! I haven't any friends here in Allison . . . no one I could confide in. Oh God, Harold would kill me if he knew I had come to you!"

Tom knew that if he didn't do something quickly to calm the woman she would have everyone in the hotel awake. Her voice was rising dangerously, and she was beginning to sob loudly.

He reached out and pulled her out of the chair, pressing her body against his own, holding her tightly while he tried to soothe her. His voice was calm and reassuring, much more so than he felt inside. He could guess only part of what had happened to the beautiful young wife, but that was enough to make his blood boil with rage. Her whole slender body shook with emotion as her tears stained his shoulder. And suddenly Tom was acutely aware that he was holding a very beautiful and desirable woman in his arms. He could feel the soft curves of her body against his own lean flesh, sense the way her nipples were pressing into him, smell the exciting aroma of her femininity.

Alarmed and embarrassed at his own reaction, at the quickening response of his desire, he tried to disengage himself from the woman. She clutched at him more tightly, making that impossible.

"Oh, please, I'm so afraid," she begged, not wanting to let go of Tom's lean and protective flesh. "There's no one else I can turn to . . . please, just hold me for a minute so I won't feel so alone!"

"No one will hurt you," he whispered, pressing his lips against her damp cheek. "I won't let them, believe me."

She nodded, shuddering with emotion. After a few minutes she relaxed and moved away reluctantly, wiping at her eyes with her handkerchief. "Will you promise me something, Mr. Cavenaugh?" she asked in an urgent whisper. "Will you promise me that you won't kill my husband . . . or anyone else?"

The words shocked Tom.

"I've no reason to kill your husband, Mrs. Cartwright," he answered. "But I intend to teach him a damned good lesson for hurting you after I warned him against it."

"No . . . you don't understand," she went on, her voice rising again. "What he did to me isn't important! I can forgive that. What I can't forgive is what my husband and those horrible friends of his did to your *brother*!"

"What are you saying?" Tom demanded.

"Your brother didn't do those awful things to Maria," Amy sobbed, "Harold as much as admitted that to me tonight before he . . . before he . . ."

"Before he slapped you around?" Tom asked, finishing the sentence for her. His own hands were trembling now, and his heart thudded violently against his chest.

"I told you, that part isn't *important*," Amy went on tearfully. She quickly told Tom after the visit of Marcus Owens that evening, how she had come downstairs and listened at the parlor door for a few minutes, how she had overheard the two men's cryptic references to the death of Maria Gomez and its aftermath, including Owens and her husband arguing about whose *fault* it was that they were now both in such a precarious position. "It didn't make much sense," Amy went on, "and I couldn't really understand why they were both so frightened of what you would find out."

She paused for a moment to dry her eyes again, then continued. Tom listened intently, his fists clenched so tightly that his nails were digging painfully into the roughened flesh of his palms.

"After Harold accused me of eavesdropping on them and ordered me upstairs, I began to wonder what it all meant. It was like some sort of nightmare! Harold screaming at me and . . . and the way he's changed since Maria's murder. At first I thought it was just the shock of him finding her like that. But, it's more than that . . . it's like he was a different person than the man I married!"

Nothing Amy Cartwright had said so far was proof that Billy had been innocent. Tom wanted desperately to have her get to the point, but he forced himself to remain quiet, letting her tell the story in her own way.

"Harold came upstairs after a while," she went on. "He came into my bedroom and started berating me again . . . repeating his accusations about me snooping on him. I tried to tell him I hadn't really done that, but he refused to listen to me. Then he said things that were even worse! Things I can't repeat to you or anyone else . . . personal abuse of me! I'm afraid I got hysterical and terrified at the same time . . . I told him what I'd overheard downstairs and demanded to know why he and Marcus Owens were so afraid of your questions, and why Jeb Fallon had run off when he heard you were in Allison. Oh, God, it was awful then. Harold became livid. He swore at me, using words so foul and disgusting that I thought he'd lost his senses. He cursed me, saying the matter was none of my business . . . *that your brother deserved to die even if he hadn't killed Maria*! That Billy and his kind were scum . . . not fit to live in the same world with decent people! I was stunned, Mr. Cavenaugh, believe me. I'd never heard my husband talk like that before. He stormed around the room throwing things and ranting and raving like an insane person, boasting that no one could ever prove that your brother was innocent of killing Maria, or connect him to Billy's lynching! When I told him that I'd tell people what he and those other men had done, Harold just laughed crazily and said a wife couldn't testify against her husband . . . and that if I told anyone he'd . . . he'd use his influence to have me committed to an insane asylum!"

"What happened then?"

"He began beating me," she whispered, the tears starting again as her body began shaking violently. "He was like a madman! Oh, God, I don't even want to think about it."

"Please tell me *everything*," Tom ordered.

"No, I can't, it's too . . . too *personal*!" she moaned, turning away from him. "When he finally left me and went downstairs again I knew I couldn't stay there another minute. I got dressed and went out the back way . . . I didn't know where to go or what to do . . . I was so frightened! Then I thought that you might help me and I came here. No one saw me and the lobby was empty when I came in. I got your room number from the register. You *will* help me, won't you? Please, you're my only hope . . . I've got to get away before he finds me!"

Tom reached out and turned her gently around so that she was facing him again. "I'll help you, Mrs. Cartwright," he said earnestly. "But I can't make any promise not to make your husband and the others pay for what they did to Billy. I want you to stay here in my room until I get back. You'll be safe."

"Where are you going?" she cried out, clutching at his arms as if trying to keep him from leaving.

"To find your husband," Tom said, gently but insistently pushing her away. "I've got to know the truth . . . and he's the only one who can give that to me."

"No, stay here with me!" she begged, throwing her arms around Tom and pressing herself against him. She knew what he would do to her husband, and the thought terrified her. No matter how much she despised Harold for what he had done to her, the thought of another killing sent shivers of revulsion through her whole body. "Please," she whispered, "please don't leave me now. Wait until tomorrow, at least. I'm so frightened . . . and I need someone to hold me and tell me everything is going to be all right . . ."

Her voice trailed off as she looked up at Tom Cavenaugh. Part of what she said was true enough, she *did* need this rugged man's strength and courage to help her through the night. He wasn't like the other men she had known—crude, leering males who made her feel dirty when they looked at her with lust written all over their faces. No, Tom Cavenaugh was different. He was as quiet and strong and self-assured as her own husband was loud and brutal. Tom was the kind of man who could protect her and make her feel wanted—wanted for her whole being, not just as an object of obscene lust.

A warm glow was beginning to spread in her loins and out through her trembling thighs and stomach as she pressed her body more tightly against him. A voice in the back of her mind sent out warnings of danger, but Amy ignored it, caught up in the wonder of desire for this man who was little more than a stranger. Her nipples tingled as they had when she touched them with her own fingers, making her knees go weak, her heart pound in her chest.

Suddenly she knew she wanted Tom Cavenaugh—wanted him to make love to her, wanted him to wash away all the hurt and humiliation she had experienced at the hands of her husband. She longed to feel his naked flesh next to her burning thighs and breasts, yearned for the exciting sensations she had only been able to dream about in the past.

Despite himself, Tom couldn't resist his own desire. He knew he should leave her and go and find her husband, but he couldn't force himself to push the lovely female away again. The other will wait, he told himself, losing himself in the overwhelming need for her.

Before either of them could stop they were kissing hungrily, their lips pressed together in steadily mounting lust. Oh, God, I shouldn't! Amy's bewildered brain cried out. Yet she was as powerless as Tom to stop the surging wave of desire that swept over them. It was like something out of her wild, erotic childhood fantasies, and she found herself running her frenzied hands over his lean, hard body.

Then they were undressing one another, pulling at each other's clothing in a desperate need to be naked and free. The beautiful young wife shivered when she felt his warm lips lovingly caress the already hardened tips of her tingling nipples. In a moment they were on the bed and she felt vibrantly alive, her naked body trembling with eager anticipation, anxious to give this man all the love she had kept bottled up inside her for so many years.

"Hurry," she called out to him in an urgent voice that was full of frantic desire.

Tom pulled himself up and began to spread her soft thighs gently apart, rolling over between them, his hardness grazing along the furry mouth between the pink flesh. Taking his own penis into his hand, Tom brought it down, pressing it against his lover's achingly sensitive clitoris and bringing a gasp of ecstasy from her lips. The exciting touch of flesh against flesh sent a tremor of throbbing lust spreading in warm, wet waves through her loins.

She could feel her vagina flowering open to him. Her hands went up to reach around his back and pull him down atop her. "Now!" she pleaded. "Oh, God, make love to me *now*!"

Nothing in Amy's past prepared her for the hurricane of pleasure that swept through her whole body when Tom entered her. She could feel her insides clutching at him, pulling him further in, contracting around the hardened male flesh. With a barely suppressed scream of animal delight, she felt her long legs come up and then close around his back, forcing him further up inside her. There was a momentary stab of pain from the brutal way Tom took her, but that was soon gone, replaced by the exquisite sensations that he brought to the writhing young wife, sensations more overwhelming than anything she had imagined possible.

She cried out in pleasure as her newly aroused passions floated free for the first time, lifting her out of her conscious control, her long-repressed sensuality exploding with a soul-shuddering excitement until she was nearly out of her mind with passion. She ground herself up to meet Tom's powerful thrusts, sucking him greedily into her upturned belly, twisting her naked hips back and forth until she was panting under the hammering of his body.

Tom's hairy chest ground into her lust-swollen breasts, massaging her straining nipples and sending new shivers of delight pounding through her lust-quaking flesh. It was almost as if her body had been made expressly for this fascinating and pleasure-giving man. Involuntarily her vaginal muscles contracted around his penis when he pulled back for the next thrilling lunge downward, caressing him, milking him, trying to draw him back into her with a sensation so wonderful that Amy couldn't believe what was happening to her.

Her sharp nails raked along his back, but the pain didn't bother Tom. He was lost in his own sexual wonderland, and he thrust in and out savagely, his lover's cries and gasps of pleasure only spurring him to new heights of desire.

When the first orgasm shook her, the beautiful young wife thought she was going to die from the intensity of the pleasure she felt. She cried out uncontrollably, wondering if any woman in the world had ever felt so much ecstasy. The next spasm shot through her quivering loins at the same time as Tom's penis began filling her belly with a warm, wet sensation of pure rapture. On and on the exquisite contractions came until Amy was limp with wonder and delight.

Tom paused for a moment to get his breath, then began pounding into her again, filling her belly with fire once again. The room was filled with the sounds of his flesh beating against her willing body, and the aromas of their lust-consumed bodies brought a new excitement to each.

At some point in their insane quest for pleasure,

Amy faintly remembered Tom pausing for a moment to pull her body around so that she was kneeling on the bed in front of him. There was no conscious sense of movement, nor any recollection of him removing his hardened shaft from her wildly-clenching belly.

What is he going to do? she wondered idly, too caught up in her own lust to protest anything he wanted of her. She felt his strong hands gripping her buttocks, then gave a gasp as he drove himself far up inside her totally vulnerable vagina. For a moment she wondered if the racing pole of pleasure was ever going to stop. But it did. And when his hairy loins were grinding lewdly against her trembling buttocks she responded automatically, pushing back against him, rotating her buttocks around and around in helpless passion as she gasped with uncontrollable joy.

She was deliriously happy, almost insane with delight when the orgasms rocked her again. This time it seemed to go on for hours. When it seemed she couldn't bear any more of the maddening pleasure, she felt him rolling over onto his back and pulling her atop him, crushing her breasts down against his mouth as his penis slid up into the wet, furry mouth between her thighs.

It was almost thirty minutes later when she finally collapsed down against him, too exhausted to move. Every nerve in her lovely young body felt alive with the after-glow of complete satisfaction. Moaning, she kissed his face and eyes as she held him tightly.

"Thank you," she whispered, her voice filled with the wonder of having become a woman at last. "Oh, God, I never dreamed it could be like this . . ."

They lay there, locked together, each of them lost in their own thoughts. Finally, after a long time, Tom was aware that the woman had fallen asleep. She gave a cry of protest when he gently slipped out from beneath her. Tom quickly wrapped his arms around her again as he pulled the covers up around their naked bodies. When she was breathing deeply in sleep again, he got out of the bed and dressed as quietly as he could. Now that his passion was satiated, his thoughts returned to Harold Cartwright. Hoping that Amy wouldn't awake until he was back, Tom grabbed up his boots and padded silently across the room to the door. Outside, in the corridor, he took his room-key from his pocket and locked the door, then slipped on his boots.

It was almost three-thirty when he went through the deserted lobby and out into the cool night air. All of his previous weariness was gone now, replaced by a grim determination to find Amy Cartwright's husband. This time the banker would talk to him, Tom vowed, and all the lies would be stripped away until only the truth was left for him to see.

He strode down the empty street toward the edge of town, moving more quickly the closer he got to the banker's house. His lean face was grim, his mouth hard, his eyes full of fury.

Chapter Six

The Cartwright house, a large Victorian building with turrets and gingerbread scrolls in the current style, sat about five hundred yards distant from Allison proper. The banker had chosen the location because of the privacy it afforded, and because he felt the isolation from the "common" people of the town gave him a kind of princely status. It was by far the most imposing home in northern Arizona.

The house was dark and silent when Tom arrived. He made a quick inspection, looking for doors or windows that might have been left unlocked and would make his entry easier. He had no intention of simply rapping on the front door and summoning Harold Cartwright. He wanted the element of surprise on *his* side, not the banker's. There were three other buildings on the property—a moderate-sized barn/stable, a smaller storage building of some kind, and what appeared to be the small wooden building used as a laundry-house.

By the time he completed his surreptitious tour he had found that all the windows and doors were locked except for an upstairs window over the building extension that housed the kitchen. It would have to do, he told himself, pulling himself up onto the kitchen roof and slowly raising the window. It opened onto the main second-story corridor. Slipping inside, Tom paused long enough for his eyes to adjust to the darkness. The only sound he heard was the monotonous ticking of a clock somewhere. Then, moving slowly and quietly, he started down the hallway, opening each doorway and peering inside. He had no trouble indentifying the different bedrooms: Amy's was furnished with graceful, imported pieces, accented by frilly lace curtains, and giving off the tantalizing aroma of her exciting perfume. There were several disused guest bedrooms, the furniture covered with dust-sheets. At the end of the hallway, next to the imposing bathroom, was the banker's bedroom/study.

Tom was sorely disappointed when he found the room empty. Cursing silently, he retraced his steps back down the corridor to the broad staircase that wound its way down to the large foyer. His boots made no sound on the carpeted stairs when he descended. From what he could see, there was a large dining room, a sewing room, and the parlor, all opening off the entryway. He quickly checked the first two, then moved over to the parlor and stood in the open doorway.

A triumphant smile creased his face when he saw the shape of a man's body on the overstuffed couch. He watched for a moment, seeing the man's chest rise and fall in sleep, then heard the almost silent softness of the man's breathing.

So I've got you, Mr. Cartwright! Tom said silently, easing his revolver from his holster as he crept across the fifteen feet that separated him from the man on the couch. Tom failed to see the small footstool that sat in front of one of the chairs. His booted foot caught the stool squarely, knocking it over with a loud clatter.

Damn! Tom swore, cursing his clumsiness.

The figure on the couch suddenly sat up, knocking the blanket which had covered him to the floor. "Who's that?" he cried out. "Harold? Is that you?"

The two men stared at one another for a split-second and then Tom leaped forward, shoving his gun into the man's face menacingly. "Don't move," he warned.

"You just sit there and don't make one goddamned false move, mister!"

"Oh, Jesus, please, don't shoot me," a terrified voice answered.

Tom grabbed up a lamp from a nearby table and thrust it into the man's hand. "Light that," he ordered, pulling a match from his shirt pocket. "Go on, light it and be quick about it!"

Marcus Owens' hands were shaking so badly he almost dropped the lamp before he finally managed to get the kerosene wick going. When the light did eventually flare up, Tom gasped in surprise.

"Owens! What in the hell are you doing out here? And where's Cartwright?"

Owens was no less shocked than Tom Cavenaugh. His eyes widened in fear when he saw the gun in Tom's hand. It was pointed directly at his head.

"Don't shoot me . . . for the love of God, don't kill me!" he begged, his voice whining and piteous.

"Answer my questions, then!" Tom warned.

Owens was torn betwen the fear of death at the hands of the grim-faced man who stood in front of him, and the certainty that—should he tell Tom Cavenaugh the truth—Harold Cartwright would see to it that his days on earth were marked. It was a terrible choice for the cowardly storekeeper. After a few seconds of soul-searching, Owens chose to deal with the immediate danger rather than the future threat.

"Cartwright went into town to find his wife," Owens swore to Tom. "They had an argument tonight and she ran off."

"You're a goddamned liar!" Tom shouted, enraged at the other man's prevarication. "I just came from town and there was no sign of Cartwright. Where is he, you bastard?"

"I'm telling the truth . . . you've got to believe me, Cavenaugh! He said if he couldn't find her, he was going to ride out to Jim Conroy's ranch and get some of Jim's boys to help look for her!"

Owens' face got even more paler and sweat began to pour off his chubby face when he saw Tom pull back the hammer of his pistol. "I'll give you one more chance and then you're a dead man, Owens," Tom said ominously. "Why did he go out to the Conroy place in the middle of the night?"

The other man suddenly broke down completely, absolutely certain that Tom was about to pull the trigger of his gun and blast him into eternity.

"No! Wait! I'll tell you . . . don't kill me! Cartwright went out to get Conroy and his men . . . they're going to ride back in and finish you off once and for all. They'll do it, too, I swear it! Harold went crazy after he and his wife had that argument and she ran off . . . he said it was all *your* fault . . . that Amy was going to talk you into running off with her! Jesus, mister, you don't know Harold like I do. He's crazy jealous about that woman . . . always accusing her and every man she talks to of cheating on him! You better get out of here while you got the chance! He'll kill you, Cavenaugh . . . he and that Conroy bunch will shoot you down like a dog! Go on, you get out of Allison . . . I won't even tell them you were here, honest to Christ, I won't!"

"Thanks," Tom said sarcastically. "But, I'm not leaving here until I know what happened the night Maria Gomez was killed. You're going to tell me, Owens. I've killed a good many men in my days . . . some of them I hated, some of them I didn't even know. Putting a bullet through that black heart of yours is going to give me the kind of pleasure none of those other killings did!"

"Tell you *what*?" Owens pleaded, trying to buy time for himself. "I told Miles Townsend everything I know, I swear to God, I did. Your brother killed that girl

. . . we just heard the screaming and found her! You can't murder me for *that*!"

Tom was growing impatient.

"I already *know* Billy didn't kill Maria Gomez," Tom said heatedly. "Cartwright admitted that to his wife before he knocked her around tonight. And Amy also overheard you and Cartwright arguing about who was to blame for what happened to Maria! Damn it, man, don't take me for a fool."

Owens' hands came up to cover his face. He began shaking violently as the hoarse sobs started. "Oh, God . . . I told him it wouldn't work . . . that you'd find out! All right, I'll tell you . . . just don't kill me, Cavenaugh! Promise you won't shoot me!"

"I'll promise you only that you'll be in hell quickly if you don't spit it out, Owens!"

"All right!" Owens screamed. "It was Jeb Fallon and Harold to blame, not me! I didn't want to hurt her . . . you've got to believe me, they talked me into it, Cavenaugh! Oh, Jesus, I wish I'd never come out here that night . . ."

"What do you think, boys?" Jim Conroy asked, an evil grin on his wrinkled and unshaven face as he looked around at the men crowded around the bunkhouse, then back over at Harold Cartwright. "Do you reckon we should help the banker here shoot this Cavenaugh dude?"

"And Miles Townsend, too, while we're at it, daddy!" Carl Conroy cried out, nodding vigorously. "It was Miles that arrested me and Will!"

"We owe it to J. R. and Emil to settle the score, Mr. Conroy," another man added. "And I ain't too happy about the men who were in that fucking posse out here tonight. I say teach the whole goddamned town a lesson while we're at it!"

"No! Cavenaugh's the one I want killed," Harold Cartwright protested quickly. "Get him out of the way and you can deal with Townsend and the others later, after things die down."

Jim Conroy scratched his head slowly while he thought over the matter. Killing Tom Cavenaugh didn't bother him, any more than having his men instigate the lynching of Billy Cavenaugh had. What concerned the half-crazy old rancher was the price he could exact from Harold Cartwright in return for his help. The matter of his new loan had already been settled the day after Billy's death at the hands of the lynch mob. Now, seeing the desperation in the face of the banker, Conroy realized that he could name his own price for his help.

Suddenly, he stood up.

"You boys catch an hour's sleep and then get ready to ride into Allison," he told his menl "We'll go in at first light and catch the fucker sleeping."

Motioning toward the door, the rancher and the banker went outside, walking slowly back toward the main house. "I've been thinking about buying the Maxwell place when it comes on the market, Cartwright," Conroy told the banker as they walked. "It's prime land and I could use the extra grazing. What do you think, Harold?" he asked slyly. "Would you be willing to lend me the money at say . . . *half* the going interest rate?"

It's goddamned blackmail! Cartwright thought bitterly, silently cursing the rancher. But he knew he would make the loan, no matter how much his penurious heart suffered as a consequence. He needed Conroy and his brutish men, and no cost was too much to pay for the death of Tom Cavenaugh. The banker's hands shook as he thought of his own hatred for the other man. And, in his irrational mind, all of his troubles could now be traced directly to the arrival of Tom Cavenaugh in Allison. Damn his soul! Cartwright cursed silently. It would give him magnificent pleasure when he could look down on the lifeless corpse of his enemy, and know that the cause of all his misery was dead.

"All right, Conroy, you'll get the money for the Maxwell Ranch," he said in surrender. "But only if I get to see that bastard Cavenaugh die . . . do you understand?"

"What about that purty little wife of yours?" Conroy cackled, twisting the verbal knife in the banker. "You going to kill her, too, for running off on you?"

Cartwright cursed again, mentally kicking himself for telling Conroy about Amy fleeing. It had been a mistake, one that the rancher wouldn't let him forget. In his insane rage, Cartwright had blurted out the whole sordid mess to Conroy—his insane jealousy of his wife, his maddening suspicions that she was betraying him with other men. The banker's fevered brain burned with sickening, ugly images of his wife in some other man's arms. The thought of her beautiful young flesh being caressed by another male drove him into another frenzy of insane rage.

"Mind your own goddamned business, Conroy!" Cartwright cried out, shaking violently as he turned to the lewdly grinning rancher. "You just take care of Cavenaugh! I'll handle my wife myself!"

"Why, sure, Harold," Conroy cackled mirthlessly again. "I was just curious, that's all." They had reached the main house. "Come on, let's open us a bottle of bourbon and shoot the shit while we wait for the sun to come up, huh? Or are you figuring to go back into town?"

"No, I'll wait and ride in with you and the men," Cartwright said sullenly, still furious with Conroy.

They went inside.

"Harold invited Jeb and me out to play poker that night," Marcus Owens told Tom, beginning slowly. "His wife Amy had taken the stage down to Prescott for some shopping, and he said he'd be alone and wanted company. I didn't get there until late, and Harold and Jeb were already half-drunk . . ."

. . . It was almost eight-thirty before Marcus finished up at the store, had his supper, and then walked out to the Cartwright house. As soon as the banker opened the door for him, Marcus could see from the expression on Harold's face that this wasn't to be an ordinary evening of poker. For one thing, Cartwright seemed to have been drinking more than he usually did. For another, the banker seemed mysteriously excited about something as he led Marcus into the dining room where Jeb Fallon waited. Several opened bottles of whiskey and brandy sat on the table, along with stacks of poker chips and decks of cards. Like Harold, Jeb Fallon was grinning cryptically as he toyed with his drink. Fallon was a thin, grey-haired man of forty. The material success he had gained had done nothing to polish his natural crudeness.

"Well, Marcus," Jeb called out to the newcomer. "Come in and fix yourself a drink. Did Harold tell you yet?"

"Tell me what?" Marcus asked, pouring himself a bourbon. "What are you two up to? You look like the cats who've eaten the canary."

"Oh, it's better than that," Fallon laughed drunkenly. "Our friendly banker has got a real treat in store for us tonight, haven't you, Harold? Yes, sir, Marcus, this is going to be an evening you'll never forget!"

"Cut out all the horseshit and tell me what's going on," Marcus complained, looking back and forth between his two friends. "I came out here to play poker, not to play stupid guessing games."

Harold Cartwright laughed uproariously at his friend's wit. "This isn't any game, my friend," he grinned lewdly. "You know how you two are always on to me about that little greaser girl who works for my wife? How you're always teasing me about getting a little bit on the side when Amy isn't looking?"

Marcus nodded, still puzzled. The subject of Maria Gomez was a standing joke between the three men. Neither Marcus nor Jeb could believe that their friend could be around the sexy young girl without seducing her—beautiful wife or not. And, like every other man in Allison, Jeb and Marcus had had those same excitingly obscene fantasies about themselves and the girl.

"Don't leave me hanging, Harold," Marcus said impatiently. "Go on, for God's sake!"

"Well, sir, neither of you two would believe me when I swore I wasn't screwing Maria," Harold went on, sipping at his brandy. "Not that I didn't want to, mind. Hell, my pecker gets hard every time I see those two beautiful titties bouncing around, and her swinging that sweet little ass of hers back and forth. And, I tried, gentlemen . . . I tried every damned way I knew how to talk that girl into letting me screw her. She just laughed and called me a hard-up *gringo*! I even offered the little slut money, and you boys know how much I hate to part with a dollar."

"You mean you finally did it?" Marcus asked in amazement, shocked by the banker's candor. "Jesus, Harold, how was she?"

"No, sir, I don't mean that at all," Cartwright laughed, rolling his eyes lewdly. "Not *yet*, at least!" He paused for effect, then went on again. "Juan Gomez came into the bank the day before yesterday . . . he's the thin mean-looking brother. The bastard had the nerve to ask me to loan him two hundred dollars! Can you imagine that . . . me loaning the bank's hard-earned money to greaser pimps? He had some cock-and-bull story about wanting the money to fix up that greaser whorehouse that they run. I told the bastard where he could get off, believe me. Then I got to thinking . . . maybe if I did Juan a favor he'd do me one. You know, one hand washing the other. Well, sir, I told him about Maria playing hard to get and always running off when I'd get her alone in the house . . ."

"She's a little prick-tease, that one," Marcus nodded.

". . . Juan, he just give me one of those shit-eating grins and says I don't know how to handle the little whore," Harold went on excitedly. "He said you've got to treat greaser women hard, to knock them around a little if they got sassy, show 'em who's boss. He said Maria used to act the same way with his brother Antonio when he started screwing her, but that Antonio soon took her down a peg and made her like it!"

"You mean her own damned *brother* was fucking her?" Marcus gasped.

"That's what the man told me," the banker nodded. "He said Antonio broke her in when she was about twelve. Well, now, boys, that sure threw me for a loop, I can tell you. Before I could say anything more, Juan kind of smiled again and asked me how I'd like him to put the fear of God into his sister . . . you know, so she'd spread those legs of hers for *me*! Hell, he wasn't fooling me none, acting like he was going to do me any favor. He wanted my two hundred dollars. We kind of dickered back and forth a while and finally settled on the loan and twenty dollars to boot. I fixed it up for Amy to go down to Prescott tonight so that Juan could come out and do his stuff."

Cartwright sat back in his chair with a smug, self-satisfied grin on his face. "Jesus," Marcus gasped. "You lucky devil, you!"

"Shit, Marcus," Jeb Fallon interrupted. "Harold fixed it up so we could all *three* have the girl!"

Marcus Owens could hardly believe his ears. The thought of having the lovely young Mexican girl was enough to send his blood racing. For a moment he thought it was all a joke on him. Frowning, he cursed Jeb and Harold for their cruel sense of humor.

"No, it's true. Marcus," Jeb assured him. "The poker game was only an excuse to get you and I away from our old women. Just think, boys, as soon as that greaser gets here we're going to be screwing some of the sweetest pussy in the whole damned Arizona Territory!"

"What time is he coming?" Marcus asked excitedly.

"He'll be here before ten," Harold answered, pouring himself another drink, beaming at his friends. "I don't ever want to hear you two accuse me of not sharing the wealth, boys. To tell the truth, I thought about keeping her all to myself, but then I figured, what the hell, we've been friends too long for that."

No one had any interest in playing poker as they waited for Juan's arrival. The talk turned more obscene as the evening wore on, with each of them bragging about what he was going to do to the young servant. The heat and the whiskey and the carnal delights that awaited them seemed to fill them all with an overwhelming sense of anticipation.

Finally, shortly after nine o'clock, Jeb couldn't wait any longer. He gulped down a last whiskey and stood up. "To hell with that spic," he announced. "I say we just go out and have our party without him!"

Before anyone could reply there was a knock at the front door. Telling his friends to wait in the dining room, Cartwright went quickly toward the front of the house. Jeb and Marcus waited impatiently, their lusts building. They could hear the banker conversing with someone, but were unable to make out the words. In a few minutes he was back, frowning. "That bastard held me up for another twenty dollars," he complained bitterly. "He said he hadn't figured on all three of us having his sister."

"Did you pay him?" Jeb asked apprehensively.

"It was too late to argue now," Cartwright nodded, shrugging. "He said to give him ten minutes and then to come on out. Jesus, boys, think of it! That little greaser is going to turn out to be a real firecracker, I know it!"

They waited as long as they could, fortifying themselves with more alcohol. Finally, unable to control themselves, they each grabbed up a bottle of whiskey and hurried out through the back door to Maria's quarters. The girl lived in a plain wooden building about ten by twelve feet, less than a twenty yards from the main house. They could see the light of her kerosene lamp through the building's single window.

"Juan!" Cartwright called out, his words slurred from the amount of brandy he had drunk. "Here we come, *amigo*!"

He pushed open the door and went inside, followed by his two drunken friends. Juan Gomez stood next to the small bed on which his terrified sister lay, a grin on his swarthy face, a knife in his hand. Maria Gomez seemed stunned when she saw the men. She was lying outside the covers, her olive-hued flesh covered only by a thin cotton nightdress that Amy Cartwright had given her. She started to scream but her cries were quickly cut off by her brother's hand over her mouth.

Juan said something harsh in Spanish, brandishing his knife under the girl's face as he spoke. When he finally pulled his hand away, Maria was wide-eyed with horror, but said nothing.

"I have told Maria what is expected of her," Juan smirked. "She has never had three such fine looking *hombres* at the same time, señor, and is a little fearful, you understand. "But I have convinced her that you mean her no harm, and that she must do as you say." He paused for a moment when Maria gave a shriek of alarm. Using his open hand, Juan slapped the girl as hard as he could, knocking her back down onto the bed. Speaking in Spanish, he threatened to use his knife on her if she didn't let the three *gringos* have what they wanted. She was shaking with fear when Juan turned back to the three men. "She is coy, this one," he laughed. "I'll leave you now, señors, unless you want me to stay."

The banker thrust his bottle into Juan's hand and pushed him outside. "We don't need you, greaser!" he shouted. "You go out in front of the house and keep your eyes open . . . we don't want any unexpected company."

"As you wish, señor," Juan replied, disappearing into the darkness.

As soon as her brother was gone Maria screamed again and made a wild dash for the window, frantically trying to throw it open.

"Get her, for Christ's sake!" Fallon shouted, rushing toward the girl. He and Marcus Owens reached Maria at the same time, grabbing her arms and legs and pulling her back toward the bed. She fought like a tigress, screaming and cursing, trying desperately to get away from the hands that were pulling her down.

In a moment she was on the bed again and her nightdress was being ripped away. She cringed, trying to cover her naked young flesh from the devouring eyes, pleading for them to go away and leave her alone.

Cartwright leaned over the bed and snarled. "Listen, you greaser slut! I paid good money to your brother and we aim to get what we paid for, *understand*? If you can spread your legs for Antonio, that pig brother of yours, you sure as hell as do the same for white men!"

"No! Please, señor Cartwright!" she pleaded, hardly able to believe what was happening to her. Being raped and abused by Antonio was bad enough. Having these three leering, drunken *gringos* sweating over her was too much to bear. Shrieking with terror, she began to struggle again, tearing at the men with her hands, kicking and shouting for mercy.

But the three men were too intoxicated by the alcohol and their own lusts to stop now. While Jeb and Marcus Owens held Maria down, Cartwright stripped off his clothing and climbed up on the bed beside the girl, running his brutal hands up and down over her naked flesh while he feasted upon her with his eyes.

Maria screamed again when he pried her legs open and began to fondle the dark triangle between them. "No, please, señor . . . I beg you!"

"Hold her, boys," the banker ordered, his saliva dripping down onto Maria's breasts. He positioned himself between her legs while his friends struggled to keep the girl quiet. Then, with a savage grunt of desire, he thrust himself down, driving his hard penis into the girl's body. He ignored her shrieks and cries of horror and pain, pumping out his obscene lusts while Jeb and Marcus urged him on.

When it was over, they changed positions, with Cartwright grabbing Maria's arms while Jeb Fallon raped her. The only sounds that came from Maria now were low moans of agony as she closed her eyes and clenched her teeth and tried to shut out her mind to the horror that was being committed upon her naked flesh.

There seemed no end to the orgy of sex and violence. Each time one of the men pulled away another took his place. Then, with one last desperate burst of energy, Maria tried to escape again when Owens was rolling off her body, his lusts temporarily satiated.

She pulled herself upright, screeching obscenities in Spanish, using her sharp nails to try to rake along the banker's forearm and force him to loosen his grip on her shoulders.

Cartwright yelled in pain and surprise. Cursing the girl, he grabbed at her head, managing to curl his fingers cruelly in her long hair. "Damn you!" he swore, balling his fist involuntarily and smashing it into the girl's face.

The blow stunned her, cutting off any further struggles. She fell back on the bed, dazed, her whole lower body filled with excruciating pain. "Get a rope," the banker ordered angrily. "Let's hog-tie this little hellion!"

In a few moments Maria's hands and feet were tied to the bed posts, her body totally vulnerable now. There was nothing she could do except lay there and endure the obscene carnage that began again immediately. On and on it went until she was beyond any sensation. Her whole body was one mass of pain, her mind almost gone from the incredible brutality being inflicted upon her.

Now that the girl was helpless, the men resumed their drinking while they watched one another taking the girl. As their drunkeness increased, new cruelties came to their alcohol-inflamed minds. It was Jeb Fallon who suggested that it was a shame to waste the girl's mouth. Grinning crazily, he climbed up onto the bed and sat atop her breasts, forcing her to take his penis between her lips.

Then it was the other men's turn, and their lusts were renewed at this obscenely exciting game. The bed was a wild jumble of naked bodies and animal-like cries of pleasure as they took her again and again. There was no resistance left in the girl. All she could do was moan in agony and disbelief as the male bodies changed positions and inflicted more pain upon her already tortured and battered flesh.

Finally, mercifully, their passions abating, the men pulled away one by one. Jeb Fallon collapsed on the bed beside the girl's still body while the banker and Marcus Owens sat down on the floor and swilled down more drink as they panted for breath and grinned mindlessly at one another.

"Jesus, I'm exhausted," Owens complained.

"Yeh, same here," Cartwright nodded, adding, "and *hungry*, too! Let's go inside and get something to eat . . . there's a ham and some fresh-baked bread in the pantry." He looked up at his friend on the bed. "What about it, Jeb? You want something to eat?"

Fallon didn't even open his eyes when he answered. "No, you go on. I'll wait for you here."

Laughing drunkenly, Marcus and Cartwright slipped on their clothing and went outside into the darkness of the night. They were shocked to find Juan and Antonio Gomez arguing heatedly near the back of the house.

"What in the fuck is *he* doing here?" Cartwright demanded, pointing to Antonio.

The younger of the two brothers smiled apologetically and shrugged. "My brother discovered I was coming out to see you and became suspicious," Juan replied. "He insisted that I tell him about our little, uh, *arrangement*. Now he wants money, as well, señor Cartwright."

"For the honor of my family!" Antonio interrupted angrily. "You have taken my sister's virtue! I demand payment, señor. Otherwise I shall speak to the authorities!"

"To hell with you, you greaser bastard!" Marcus Owens replied loudly. "Your brother said you screwed her yourself! You ain't blackmailing us, damn it!"

"Lies . . . he lies!" Antonio screamed. "My sweet

sister was chaste before this night! I demand payment for this dishonor you have brought upon her . . ."

Before anyone could reply to Antonio's cynical words, they heard a scream coming from Maria's quarters. The shriek was ear-splitting, the sound of someone in the throes of horror. Then another, this one louder than the first.

"Jesus Christ, what's he doing to her?" Marcus Owens roared.

The two Gomez brothers looked at one another uneasily.

"Come on, Marcus," Cartwright ordered, turning toward the direction of Maria's cries. "You blackmailing goddamned greasers stay here. We'll take care of this!"

But the Gomez brothers had no intention of staying behind. They followed the banker and Marcus Owens across the yard. The girl's screeches were becoming more and more frantic now. Then, just as they reached the small building, the cries stopped as suddenly as they had begun.

But they could now hear the angry voice of Jeb Fallon shouting. "Shut up, damn you! Stop that yelling, bitch!"

Alarmed, the four men pushed their way into the small room, wide-eyed at the sight that greeted them. Jeb Fallon was sitting atop the girl's chest, his hands around her neck, shaking Maria violently while he cursed and screamed at her.

"Oh, *Dios*!" Juan gasped, crossing himself hurriedly. "He has *killed* her!"

His sister's lifeless eyes and dark, protruding tongue was mute testimony to the accuracy of his words. Shuddering with horror, Marcus and Cartwright grabbed at their friend, trying desperately to pull him away from the girl. It took all their combined strength to shake loose his hands. Fallon's eyes were wild and demented, and he fought them off as best he could.

Finally, seeing that Jeb was totally irrational, Marcus Owens balled his fist and struck the man as hard as he could. Fallon collapsed on the floor alongside the bed.

"Murderer!" Antonio Gomez shrieked, trying to push his way past the other to get to Jeb Fallon. "Oh, my poor sister! I'll kill you, you *gringo* pig!"

Suddenly the small room was an exploding mass of twisting, writhing bodies as Juan Gomez grabbed his brother around the neck and attempted to pull him outside. At the same time, Cartwright and Marcus Owens tried to protect their fallen friend from the Mexican's fury.

Juan finally managed to quiet his brother. He stood over Antonio, threatening the sobbing man with a wicked-looking knife.

"Oh, Jesus, what are we going to do, Harold?" Marcus Owens asked, wringing his hands as he looked down at the dead girl on the bed. Her neck had been snapped by Jeb Fallon's fury. Her head now lay slumped over, almost at right angles to her naked body. There were bruises everywhere on the girl's flesh, and she looked terribly young and vulnerable in death.

"Shut up and let me think, damn it!" the banker snarled, his mind whirling and confused. He watched as Marcus suddenly raced to the doorway and vomited, pouring out the contents of his stomach onto the ground.

It was like a nightmare, he thought, trying desperately to shake off the effects of all the brandy he'd drunk. How could he have gotten himself mixed up in murder? he wondered bitterly. His head was pounding as he tried to think. He was ruined! They all were! What had started out to be nothing more than a few hours of sexual pleasure for them had suddenly turned into something grotesque! Horrible images flashed across his fevered brain—images of himself being arrested and tried for complicity in the girl's death, maybe even being hanged!

Oh God! he thought, I can't let that happen. Everything he had worked for gone in a moment of terrible madness! There was no sympathy for the girl lying dead on the cot, only an overwhelming desire to escape his own culpability.

"This is bad business, señor," Juan Gomez said softly, smiling mirthlessly at the banker. "You must pay my brother and I much money for our loss. This is a terrible thing you have done."

"A *terrible* thing!" Antonio Gomez said, almost in chorus. "A thousand dollars would be small compensation for such a tragedy . . . no, two thousand at least!"

Suddenly Juan Gomez signalled frantically to the others to be quiet. "I hear someone on the road," he whispered. "Stay here, all of you . . . I will see who it is."

The Mexican slipped away, gliding silently toward the house. No one else moved, but Cartwright could hear Marcus Owens sobbing softly as he tried to keep from retching again.

Almost a full minute later Juan was back.

"Who is it?" the banker asked hoarsely.

"There may be a solution to this problem, señor," Juan grinned, his voice barely above a whisper. "Would it be worth five thousand dollars to you and your friends to escape the consequences of what you have done to my poor sister?"

The amount shocked Cartwright, but he nodded eagerly.

"Stay in here then and make no sound," Juan ordered, pressing his index finger to his thin lips. "Do not come outside until I tell you, understood?"

He waited for them to agree, then slipped outside again, shutting the door behind him. It was torture for Cartwright and Marcus Owens to have to stay inside the small building with the dead girl's grotesque body only a few feet away. The seconds went by, each of them bringing new fear to the two men. They almost envied Jeb Fallon who had passed out from drink and emotion on the floor.

They stopped breathing when they heard the sounds of footsteps coming toward the building. A man's voice outside cursed when his foot kicked something and made a loud noise. Then, out of the darkness came the voice of Billy Cavenaugh.

"Maria?" Billy called out in a half-whisper, his words thick with drunkeness. "Maria, honey? It's Billy . . . unlock the door and let me . . ."

There was a thud, then the sound of a body crashing to the ground. Suddenly the door was flung open and Juan's face was peering in at them.

"Your problems are over, señors," he chuckled. "I think I have discovered who killed my poor little sister." He paused, half-turning, pointing at Billy Cavenaugh who lay unconscious in the dirt. "But first, señor Cartwright, you and I have a little business we must conduct, is that not so? A matter of five thousand dollars!"

". . . Harold and the greaser went into the house and took care of the money," Marcus Owens went on, ". . . signed a sort of note or something. Afterwards we . . . we . . ."

Tom Cavenaugh had been listening with mounting rage as the storekeeper spoke. How could supposedly civilized men do those kinds of things? he wondered, thinking about the pitiful Maria Gomez and the horror of her death. It was monstrous, almost too disgusting to believe. But he believed Marcus Owens. And he hated the man who sat there in front of him on the overstuffed settee and described the savagery he and his friends had brought the girl. And then, when the foul and disgusting deed was finished, the three men had actually conspired with the murdered girl's brothers to frame Billy for the crime! Even before her tortured and battered body was cold, they were ready to accuse an innocent man of the vicious act—a man whose only crime had been being drunk and helpless at the wrong time and in the wrong place. Not satisfied with seeing Billy legally convicted and hanged, Cartwright, Fallon, and Owens had arranged to have Billy dragged from jail and lynched like some sort of animal. It took every ounce of will power that Tom possessed not to pull the trigger of his gun and blow out the brains of Marcus Owens.

"Go on," he said at last, getting his emotions under control again. "Tell me all of it!"

"Juan and his brother fixed it up so that Billy looked guilty of killing the girl," Marcus Owens sobbed. "Me and Harold got Jeb sobered up and cooked up the story about hearing the girl's screams and going out to find her dead and your brother in bed naked with her. Oh, Jesus, it was awful . . . all the lying we had to do . . . wondering every moment was your brother going to remember what happened and expose us . . ." he paused, ". . . you've got to believe me, Cavenaugh, it was Harold Cartwright and that greaser that talked me into going along with them. And I didn't have nothing to do with your brother's lynching . . . Jeb and Harold fixed that up with Jim Conroy. I didn't even know about it until after Billy was already dead! They knew you were on your way to Allison and wanted Billy dead before you got here . . ."

Tom felt sick to his stomach. Six people dead, and all because these men couldn't control their animal passions, he thought bitterly. How many other lives would be ruined before the thing ended?

"W-w-what are you going to do to me?" Marcus Owens whispered.

"I should shoot you like the goddamned murdering coward you are," Tom answered, his heart thudding against his chest. "But, I won't. If the law doesn't hang you, I'm going to see that you spend the rest of your life at Yuma Prison. I want you to suffer twenty-four hours a day until you go to hell where you belong, Owens. And, I swear to you, on the name of my brother Billy, I'm going to come to that prison as often as I can just to see your rotting carcass and make certain you remember who put you there!"

Stunned, Owens didn't resist when Tom grabbed his

arm and pulled him to his feet. He was like a dead man already, Tom thought. How long could he survive the brutal prison? A year, two at most?

"Let's go," Tom ordered.

Owens suddenly came to life. He pulled his arm away from Tom's hand, using it to batter the gun out of Tom's fingers. Owens fell to the floor, picking up the gun almost before Tom could react. "I'm not going to your goddamned prison!" Owens screamed jamming the weapon up against the side of his face and jerking the trigger.

The deafening explosion blew off the top of Owens' head.

It was just breaking dawn when Tom left the Cartwright house and walked slowly back into Allison. Ordinarily, he loved this time of day, when everything was cool and quiet and peaceful, and a man could look around at the vast emptiness of Arizona and almost believe the beautiful land was not filled with violence and suffering.

He went past the hotel, thinking of the lovely young woman upstairs in his bed, remembering the pleasure their bodies had given one another. Before the day was out, Amy Cartwright would either be a widow or the wife of a man disgraced and in jail on charges that would shock her very soul. It would be a tragedy either way, but Amy Cartwright's suffering would be no more acute than the pain her husband had already inflicted upon so many people. Innocent people like Maria Gomez, Billy, Amos Wicklund. The others who had been drawn into the drama—Jeb Fallon and Marcus Owens, the Gomez brothers, Gilman and the ranch hand named Emil—despicable men who deserved to die.

And how many more corpses would there be? he wondered.

Tom pushed open the door of the jail, surprised to

see Miles Townsend sitting behind his desk. The deputy looked pale and tired, but he managed a smile when he saw Tom

"What in the hell are you doing up?" Tom asked. "Doc Mayberry isn't going to like this."

"Ah, I couldn't sleep," Townsend replied, shrugging. "My shoulder started hurting like the devil a while back, so I got up and made some coffee. How about you, Cavenaugh? What are you doing up this early?"

"It's a long story," Tom said, pouring himself a cup of coffee and sitting down opposite the deputy. He began slowly, telling Miles Townsend everything that had happened at the Cartwright house, leaving out only the part about Amy Cartwright coming to his room. Townsend listened, a stunned expression on his face as Tom recounted the true story of Maria's murder, then the cover-up and framing of his brother Billy, ending in the lynching of an innocent man.

"My God!" Townsend said when Tom was finished. The deputy shook his head in shock and disbelief. "It doesn't seem possible. I mean, those men were my *friends*! How in the name of everything decent could they have done something like that?" He paused, frowning. "I suppose that explains why Cartwright invited me to supper the evening Billy was lynched . . . to get me out of the way. And I fell for it like a goddamned fool! You say Marcus shot himself?"

"I guess he was afraid of prison," Tom replied, nodding. "How quick can you get the local magistrate to issue warrants for Cartwright and Jeb Fallon? As soon as the banker is in custody, I'll ride up to Ash Fork and round up that other bastard."

"I don't think you understand the situation, Cavenaugh," Miles Townsend said slowly. "We don't have any evidence against Cartwright and Fallon . . . just what a dead man told you, and some folks might even think you were making it all up just to clear your brother's name."

Tom jumped up from his chair, his face twisted with rage.

"God help anybody who says that!" he cried out, staring hard at the man across the desk. "Do *you* think I'd lie about it, Townsend?"

"No . . . hell no!" the lawman quickly assured Tom. "I'm just pointing out the facts, son. Don't worry, I'll talk to Harold and Jeb, all right, and the way I feel right now I wouldn't mind beating a confession out of the bastards. We've got to face it, though, Cavenaugh. They're not likely to admit anything."

Tom strode over to the doorway leading into the cell area. "What about Juan Gomez?" he snarled. "I can make that fucker talk!"

Townsend shook his head sadly.

"Not unless you've got a pipeline to hell, son," he said. "Juan kicked off about two o'clock, according to the doc . . . he said it was loss of blood. Sorry, Cavenaugh, but *he* ain't going to help you none."

Tom felt suddenly helpless.

It was one thing to be in the dark about Cartwright's and Fallon's complicity in Maria's murder and his brother's lynching. That was frustrating enough. But to know with a certainty that the two men were guilty of both crimes, and yet have the law powerless to act against them, that was much worse!

"I'll kill them myself," he said coldly, meaning every word.

"You'll face me if you do, Cavenaugh," the lawman warned ominously. "There's been too much bloodshed already. If Cartwright and Fallon pay for what they've done, it'll be at the hands of the law . . . not from the end of your gun! You let *me* handle this."

"It was *you* who let those murders kill my brother!" Tom reminded the deputy angrily.

The words stung Miles Townsend as much as if Tom had struck him across the face. He sat there for several moments without replying, and Tom could almost see the man aging in front of his eyes. Still, he couldn't retract the insult.

When Townsend stood up and strapped on his gunbelt, Tom almost expected the lawman was going to try and arrest him to stop any further violence. Instead, Miles smiled grimly.

"I've warned you, Cavenaugh," he said quietly, "and there's nothing more to be said. You told me that Harold Cartwright had gone out to the Conroy place to get help . . . that they're coming after you. Any idea when they'll be in?"

"Who knows?" Tom shrugged.

"Well, I'll get busy and round up some of the men to meet them," Townsend went on. It was obvious to Tom that the lawman was in no condition for a confrontation with the crazed rancher, but just as obvious that Miles had no intention of shirking what he considered to be his duty. "Stay out of my way, son, and I'll stay out of yours."

He left Tom standing in the jail, slamming the door shut behind him.

Tom hesitated for a moment and then went after the deputy, catching up with him on the street. "Wait a minute, Townsend," he called out.

The lawman stopped, waiting for Tom, a puzzled expression on his stern face. "What is it?" he asked.

"You're in no condition to handle Conroy and that gang of thugs of his," Tom said, genuinely concerned for the other man.

"I know that," Townsend replied, nodding. "There's not going to be any gunfight if I can get some men into position at the edge of town and stop them there. Conroy's men are killers and I don't want any more bloodshed, but we'll have the advantage of surprise if they want a fight. We can manage to put things off for a while, it'll give me time to get a message to Sheriff Buchanan in Prescott. The sheriff'll send men up to help me arrest Conroy and his hooligans." He paused, then went on. "Don't worry, son, those who had a hand in lynching Billy will pay for it. Not today, perhaps, but soon, I promise you."

"And Harold Cartwright?"

"We've already been through that," the lawman replied impatiently. "I'll take him in and question him. I don't think he'll admit to anything, but at least he'll start to sweat when he realizes we know what really happened that night."

Tom nodded.

"Look, Townsend, I spoke out of turn back there in the jail," he said earnestly. "I'm sorry for it. There was no way you could have known they intended to lynch Billy that night you left him alone and unguarded."

"It was my responsibility, and I take full blame for it," Townsend insisted bitterly. "You have every right to blame me for being such a fool, Cavenaugh."

"Do me a favor then and our account will be squared. Fair enough?"

"I'm not going to let you gun down Harold Cartwright," Townsend replied heatedly.

"What if he draws down on me first?"

"Why in hell would Cartwright do that?" Townsend demanded, frowning. "He's not stupid enough to challenge you in a gunfight."

"But, if he did?"

"Then you'd have a right to defend yourself, of course. Look here, Cavenaugh, what in hell are you getting at?"

"Cartwright will be coming back in with the Conroy bunch, I expect. All I want you to do is give him a message from me. If you do, I swear I'll warn the bastard unless he comes gunning for me. Is that good enough for you?"

Townsend didn't answer for several moments. He stood there staring at Tom Cavenaugh suspiciously, as if trying to figure out what kind of trick the other man was playing on him. A few minutes before, Tom had been talking about shooting down the banker without mercy. Now he seemed calm and rational. Yet, the lawman couldn't believe that Tom had given up his need to avenge his brother's death.

"What message do you want me to give Cartwright?" he asked.

"You tell the bastard his wife is over at the hotel . . . in *my* room . . . in *my* bed! If he wants her back, he'll have to come and get her."

The deputy could hardly believe his ears. Despite the banker's insane and well-known jealousy of his beautiful young wife, Townsend was as certain as anything in the world that Amy had no lovers, or had ever been unfaithful to her husband.

"What kind of goddamned foolishness if this, Cavenaugh," he growled. "Amy Cartwright isn't that kind of woman!"

"I assure you, it's the truth," Tom insisted. "She's there now . . . waiting for me to come back to her. That's what I intend to do right now. Well, will you give Cartwright my message?"

For a moment Townsend didn't reply. He looked at Tom, shaking his head with amazement. Then, suddenly, he burst out laughing.

"I'll be a sonofabitch!" he chuckled. "You're a devious bastard, Cavenaugh, and that's a fact. All right, I'll pass on your message to Cartwright. but, remember, if you draw on him first and kill him, you'll hang for it!"

"I understand," Tom nodded. "I've given you my word on that."

He turned and walked quickly toward the hotel.

Chapter Seven

The sleepy young desk clerk was behind his polished counter when Tom entered the hotel. "Morning," the man said, wondering where his guest had been all night.

"Morning," Tom replied, stopping at the counter.

"Something I can do for you?" the clerk asked.

"I may be having a visitor later this morning," Tom nodded. "I'm expecting Harold Cartwright, the banker. "Will you tell the maid not to bother with my room until he's gone? Oh, there's one more thing. I've a lady in my room . . . she came during the night. How much more do I owe you?"

The clerk was confused.

"I don't understand, Mr. Cavenaugh," he said. "What lady? Did she register?"

"I'll do that for her," Tom answered, pulling the hotel register toward him and inking in Amy Cartwright's name. He pushed the book back toward the clerk.

"That's a dollar more," the youth said, his eyes suddenly widening in amazement when he saw Amy's name written in below Tom's. "The banker's *wife* is upstairs?" he asked hoarsely. "In *your* room?"

Tom threw a silver dollar on the counter and went upstairs. The full implication of Tom's words only then struck the clerk. Amy Cartwright! he gasped aloud. It was common knowledge in Allison how jealous Harold Cartwright was of his beautiful young wife, how the banker could be sent into towering rages when any male flirted with her on the street. Jesus! he thought excitedly, we all thought she was so damned pure and here she is catting around with the brother of the man who raped and killed her maid! Worse yet, Tom Cavenaugh had told him that the banker was coming to see him sometime that very morning! If that was true, if Harold Cartwright found his lovely wife cheating on him with Tom Cavenaugh, there were going to be some real fireworks!

The youth was suddenly wide awake. He came out from behind the counter and raced into the kitchen to share his exciting gossip with the cook and any other hotel employee who might be up and about.

Before long, everyone in the hotel would know of the scandal and the impending confrontation between the banker and Tom Cavenaugh. And, not long after that, everyone in Allison would be snickering at the skinflint banker being cuckolded so outrageously, then crowding around the hotel waiting for Harold Cartwright to arrive.

Amy Cartwright was still asleep when Tom unlocked the door of his room and slipped inside, locking it behind him. She lay on her back on the bed, the covers pulled up to her chin, her golden hair fanned out around her lovely face.

Undressing quickly, Tom took his revolver from its holster and put it on the nightstand next to the bed. Amy awoke slowly when he climbed in beside her. She smiled lazily as she reached for him with her slender arms. The sheet and blanket fell away, allowing him to see the magnificence of her naked flesh for the first time in the light.

"Good morning, darling," she whispered, pressing her warm lips against his mouth and letting her hair trail over his bare shoulder. When she pulled her mouth away from his, it was only to whisper into his ear,

"Make love to me again, Tom. Please, I've been dreaming about how beautiful it was last night . . ."

Her fingers snaked down to his loins while she spoke, wrapping around the heated flesh of his penis and massaging it lovingly. They both moaned with pleasure when he gently pressed her back down onto the mattress on her back, then spread her creamy thighs open to his delighted eyes.

"It was so wonderful," she cooed, her body beginning to tremble when she felt the hardness of him pressing into her thigh. As soon as he rolled over and knelt between her long legs, Amy pulled his head down and crushed his lips against her own again. Her tongue shot out and slipped between his teeth, darting and swirling, searching for him even as her hand guided his maleness toward the waiting warmth and wetness of her pink, furry-mouthed slit between her trembling thighs. When she pulled her head away again, it fell down onto the pillow and began rolling back and forth, her eyes aimlessly staring up at him as if in a trance. Suddenly they both felt the touch of his penis against her pussy. She moaned, pulling the rubbery tip inside her, jerking her hips upward to suck him in.

Tom smiled and reached his hands down under her quivering buttocks, holding them for a moment, then pulling them up and forcing her gyrating loins against his own. Her fingernails dug into his naked shoulders and she began to undulate her hips, pressing herself savagely up as his penis sunk deeper into her belly. The clasping softness of the beautiful woman's vagina pulling and massaging at him, holding him prisoner down in the well of delicious sensation down between her wide-spread legs—all of these were making Tom hot with a furious desire. He pushed forward, burying his toes in the mattress and sinking every inch of himself into the depths of her vaginal tunnel, making her shriek with ecstasy.

She wailed again, squirming and throwing her hips up frantically to meet his driving thrusts, grinding her pelvis against the sharp bone in his groin.

With a growing rhythm he began to plunge and withdraw his throbbing shaft, feeling the contracting muscles of her pussy pull and suck wildly for more of the lust-inciting flesh. Again and again he drove himself into her, all the time watching her hard-nippled breasts and the expression of maddening pleasure written all over the woman's beautiful face. She seemed oblivious to everything but the pummeling shaft that was bringing her such joy, inwardly screaming for the rumbling torrent of the remembered orgasms, whimpering aloud at the nerve-shattering fire that seared down in her belly and spread out like warm, wet fingers of fire through her whole body.

Aflame with his own overwhelming desire for climax, Tom drove her hard, buffeting her mercilessly down on the bouncing mattress, wanting them both to remember these moments for the rest of their lives.

"Oh, oh, ohhhhh," she gasped frantically beneath him, her arms jerking limply at her sides now and her rubbery legs useless. Her mind was an endless stream of flashing lights and electric shocks piercing her straining, lust-sensitive nerves. There were only seconds left until her climax and she could feel the blood-filled muscles of her belly beginning to rumble and roll like waves in the ocean. She was on fire—ready to erupt!

Suddenly she screamed incoherently and bucked upwards, lifting him as his own climax exploded. Together they moaned in the throes of their intense sensations until finally, exhausted by the wild lovemaking, Tom let his body slip down atop hers and they lay there, neither of them wanting to move, both alive with the dancing fingers of warm pleasure that continued to roll through their panting bodies.

* * *

Miles Townsend managed to rouse fifteen sleepy men to stop Jim Conroy and his crew. Deputizing those who had not been a part of the posse the evening before, he led them about a quarter of a mile out of town, along the road to the Conroy ranch. It was an area of low hills with large boulders scattered along each side of the road, giving the men excellent cover and protection.

"I don't want any shooting if it can be avoided," he cautioned them. "If Conroy's men start it, however, shoot to kill, but only on my signal. I'm going to try and talk them into going back to the ranch without any trouble." He paused, turning to the man named McQuaid. "McQuaid, you ride up a ways and watch for any sign of them. As soon as you see 'em, skedaddle back here as quick as you can."

McQuaid nodded and moved his horse up the road.

While they waited, Miles checked the position of each of his men, then went back out into the road and lit a cigar, smoking calmly. It was still early, but already the sun was starting to beat down on the land.

About fifteen minutes later, McQuaid came racing back. He reined in his horse and slid off, his Winchester in his hand. "They're coming, Miles," he told the deputy. "I counted twelve or thirteen riders, plus someone in a buggy."

"That'll be Harold Cartwright," the lawman nodded. "All right, McQuaid, find yourself some cover. I'll wait out here. If there's trouble and I go down, you'll be in charge."

McQuaid scurried up into a rock formation, training his rifle on the road. The cloud of dust from the horses grew larger, and then, suddenly, they were in view. Conroy and his men were riding hard, closely followed by the banker's buggy. *Well, here we go, old son,* Townsend told himself, levering a shell into his rifle and throwing the butt of his cigar down into the dirt.

Jim Conroy signalled to his riders when he saw the

lawman standing in the road a hundred yards off. The group slowed, then came toward Townsend at a trot. When they were only a few feet away, the men reined in.

"What's your goddamned game, Townsend?" Jim Conroy demanded angrily.

Townsend searched the faces of the riders before answering. Sure enough, Carl Conroy, the rancher's son, and Will Hoffstader were among the group.

"I see you've brought my prisoners back," Miles said, smilling. "Well, Jim, you just turn 'em over and head on back to your ranch. I don't want you in town causing me any problems."

The old rancher shook his head in disbelief, then cackled loudly. "Why you stupid sonofabitch!" he laughed crazily. "I told you last night, you ain't putting my boy or nobody else from my crew into your fucking jail! You get out of the way or, by Jesus, I'll put a bullet in you where you stand!"

Harold Cartwright's buggy had just caught up to the riders. The banker pulled his horse up when he reached the group, a surprised look on his face.

"What's going on here, Townsend?" he growled.

"Well, Mr. Cartwright," the deputy said slowly, "I've just told this crazy old asshole that he and his men aren't coming into Allison this morning. I know what you're up to, and it isn't going to happen. You got this bastard and his men to lynch Billy Cavenaugh. Well, sir, they're not going to shoot down the man's brother . . . not if I can help it!"

"You're crazy!" Cartwright screamed. "I didn't have anything to do with that lynching. You were with me when it happened, damn it!"

"We'll talk about that later, Mr. Cartwright," Townsend replied. "That and a hell of a lot of other things . . . like who really killed Maria Gomez?" The lawman came closer to the buggy. "I've got a message for you, Mr. Cartwright . . . it's from Tom Cavenaugh."

Conroy and his riders were getting restless.

"Screw him!" the old rancher yelled down at the banker. "Come on, boys, let's get into town and find this bastard we're looking for. You coming, banker?"

"No! Wait!" the ashen-faced Cartwright ordered. He looked back at the deputy sheriff. "What's your message?"

It gave Miles Townsend a great deal of pleasure to repeat Tom's message word for word. The banker listened, stunned, then angry, then in a wild rage. Suddenly, without warning, he reached over and grabbed the rifle from Jim Conroy's saddle, cursing loudly as he threw it onto the seat of his buggy and grabbed up his whip, slashing viciously at his horse.

The startled and pained horse bolted forward, picking up speed as the buggy raced toward the town.

"Go home, Canroy," Townsend warned the rancher again.

"The hell we will!" Conroy shouted, bringing his arm up in signal for the riders to move forward again. As he did so, he snaked his Colt .44 from his holster, aiming it at Miles Townsend. "You asked for it, you stupid fucker!"

Before he could squeeze the trigger there was a loud explosion from somewhere to the right behind the rocks. Conroy's body bucked backward, then slumped forward as he slid off his horse. The animal screamed and bolted, dragging the old rancher down the road by the splindly leg caught in the stirrup. When they saw what had happened, several of the riders spurred their horses around and raced after their employer, leaving Carl Conroy and the rest of the men behind. The men appeared shocked.

"You killed my daddy!" Carl whined, reaching for his own gun. Weapons were coming out of the other holsters, too, as the riders began to react with rage.

Suddenly, before Miles could stop the carnage, the

men behind the rocks began a wild fusillade. Screams and explosions and terrified horses and the dust churned up by their rampaging hooves made it difficult to see.

Miles scrambled away, taking cover behind the closest rock outcropping. "Hold your fire, damnit!" he screamed to his men. "Hold it, for the love of God!"

Miraculously, the men were able to hear his shouted orders above the unholy din of the gunbattle. When the firing and smoke finally died down, only Carl Conroy and one other cowboy were still alive. Several of the horses were down, as well, writhing and twisting in the dirt, their piteous shrieks almost deafening.

"Don't shoot me . . . oh, Jesus, don't kill me!" Carl Conroy pleaded, throwing down his gun and raising his hands high above his head.

Sickened by what he saw, Miles Townsend called his men down from their cover. And when the gunshots rang out again, it was only to put the injured horses out of their misery.

"I just can't seem to get enough of you, darling," Amy Cartwright giggled, blushing deeply as she bent over Tom's naked body and began kissing his chest lightly. "I feel like a . . . a *whore*! And, yet, I don't care!"

Very reluctantly, Tom gently pushed her away, sitting up and facing the suddenly-puzzled woman. "What's wrong?" she cried out, blushing again. "Am I being too aggressive?"

"No, it's not that, Amy," he said with a sigh. "There's something I have to tell you . . . something about your husband and Maria Gomez."

He saw the immediate pain in the beautiful woman's eyes at the mention of Harold Cartwright. *God forgive me*, he said silently, *I wish I didn't have to hurt her any more.*

"No!" she pleaded, trying to stop him from speaking. "I don't want to hear it. Please, Tom, don't say anything more. Just take me in your arms and make love to me again. I want to feel you inside me . . . hurting me and giving me such wonderful pleasure at the same time. Please, darling, do it again the way you did it last night . . . from the back . . . hard and brutal, as if you wanted to drive yourself right through me!"

He was tempted to do as she asked, to turn her naked body around and pound into her upturned vagina until she was screaming with ecstasy. But he knew he couldn't. Not yet. Not until this thing with her husband was settled. And, he told himself sadly, she probably won't want ever to look at me after I kill him.

"It's got to be said, Amy," he told her earnestly, his face grave. "I went out this morning . . . after you'd gone to sleep. I was looking for your husband. I found Marcus Owens, instead."

"What happened?" she whispered, suddenly still.

It was one of the hardest things he had ever had to do, telling this naive and lovely wife what a monster her husband was, how Cartwright and his depraved friends had not only raped and tortured and killed Maria Gomez, but had done as she herself suspected—*conspired to murder his brother Billy.*

Amy listened with mounting horror, not speaking, her body beginning to tremble as he held her. When it was finished, she began to weep, quietly but emotionally.

"And now he wants to kill *you*?" she asked through her bitter tears. "Oh, darling, we've got to get away before he can find us! You don't know Harold . . . he's insanely jealous of me. If he even suspected we were together like this nothing would stop him from killing us both!"

"He *does* know," Tom said softly. "I asked Miles Townsend to tell him you were here in my hotel room."

Stunned, Amy Cartwright looked at Tom as if he were mad.

"But *why*?" she gasped. "Why would you do such a thing?"

"Because I *want* him to come gunning for me," Tom replied. "The law knows your husband was involved in the killing of Maria Gomez and arranged to have Billy lynched, but they can't touch him. Oh, they'll try to get him to confess, but we both know he won't do that. So a killer will go loose . . . *two* of them if you count Jeb Fallon. Don't you understand, Amy? If I don't punish him no one will."

The lovely woman pushed him away, her eyes full os self-pity and hate. "You're using me to kill my husband," she cried out. "Oh, God, how could you do this to me? What a complete and utter fool you must think I am!"

She slapped him as hard as she could across the face, leaving the marks of her fingers on his flesh. Before he could stop her, she jumped up from the bed and began gathering up her clothing, sobbing wildly as she started to dress.

"I hate you!" she screamed down at him. "You let me think you cared for me, damn you! I gave you the only thing a woman has of any value to men, my body! And all the time you were laughing at me and plotting to murder Harold with this disgusting scheme of yours!"

"Don't you want to see him punished for what he did to Maria and my brother?" Tom asked heatedly. "I admit I used you, but that doesn't mean I don't care for you, Amy."

"Liar!" she shrieked. "You just want to avenge your damned *honor*! I don't care what he did to Maria or your brother! She was just a dirty little Mexican slut who deserved what she got! And, you told me yourself, your brother was just a drunk who couldn't hold down a job or stay out of trouble. Do you think I care what happens to people like *that*?"

It was Tom's turn to be shocked. Amy's rage at him was understandable. He had, after all, used her as the bait to get back at Harold Cartwright. What was unforgiveable was her total lack of compassion for Maria Gomez and Billy—two innocent people who had been brutalized and then killed for no other reason other than they had been helpless and unable to defend themselves against Harold Cartwright's money and power.

"You don't mean that," he said urgently, getting up out of bed and facing Amy. "You're just upset with me, Amy."

"I meant every word I said!" she insisted, pushing him away. "You're animals, all of you . . . twisted, bloodthirsty animals! I thought you might be different, but you're not . . . you're as bad as the rest, violence is all you know or care about. To hell with Maria Gomez and your brother! To hell with every uncivilized, crude animal in this whole godforsaken place! And," she added, drawing herself up and spitting fire with her eyes, "to hell with you, Tom Cavenaugh!"

She turned and went quickly to the door, pulling frantically at the knob. When it didn't open, she began beating at the wooden panels with her angry fists. "Open it!" she called out to Tom hysterically. "Unlock this door!"

It was too late for that..

Tom heard the angry screams from the corridor and the sounds of running feet as Harold Cartwright raced up the hotel stairway and down the hallway toward his room.

Moving quickly, Tom ran over to the door and grabbed Amy's arm, pulling her out of danger. She swung around and tried to hit at him, using her fists like hammers in her attempt to free herself.

"Let me go, damn you!" she cursed, screeching and striking out at Tom. Her voice died out suddenly when she heard her husband's shouts of insane rage outside in the hallway. An expression of terror replaced that of hysterical rage on her face.

"Oh, my God, it's Harold!" she gasped.

Suddenly there was the thunderous sound of the banker beating on the door with the butt of his rifle. "Cavenaugh! Amy, you goddamned whore! I know you're in there, both of you! I'll kill you both . . . I swear to God, I'll kill you!"

Cartwright sounded as if all the devils of hell were inside him. He was consumed by a fury, an insane rage, an overwhelming need to kill his wife and her lover.

Tom grabbed Amy's arm again, shoving her into the corner of the room, praying she would be safe there from her murderous husband's gun. Terrified, the young wife huddled there, sobbing loudly, and mumbling incoherently.

Tom waited for the battering to stop momentarily, then called out, "What do you want, Cartwright? Your pretty little wife and I don't want to be disturbed!"

The taunting question only served to enrage the banker even more. He slammed the rifle butt into the door with a force so violent that the wood splintered.

"I'll kill you . . . by Christ, I'll kill you!"

Tom moved back toward the bed, climbing in and stretching out with his right hand only inches from the revolver on the nightstand. It seemed bizarre, even to him, to be lying there naked while a man battered at the door—a man armed with a deadly weapon and his own blind jealous fury.

In a moment the hole in the door was large enough for Cartwright to reach in and grasp the knob. His frantic fingers pulled at the steel, trying to open the door. When that failed, they went down to feel for the key. There was no key in the lock. It lay atop the dresser, several feet away.

The banker's screams of outrage were almost incoherent now as he became more and more frustrated.

Pulling his hand back outside, he pointed the rifle barrel at the lock and pulled the trigger.

The explosion was deafening as steel and wood flew in all directions. Tom waited, his heart thumping, every nerve in his body tense and alive to the danger that faced him.

Suddenly, accompanied by a loud, almost inhuman, shriek, the door burst open and Harold Cartwright raced into the room.

The banker's normally sleek face was a rage-contorted mask of insane fury. Obscenities flew from his twisted lips and his eyes were filled with hatred when he saw Tom lying calmly on the bed, a grim smile on his face.

"You bastard!" Cartwright screamed, bringing the rifle up and pointing it directly at Tom's body. "Where's my goddamned two-timing wife? You fucker! You dirty rotten prick!"

His head swung around when he heard his wife's sobs. Seeing her crouched in the corner, he screamed again, bringing the rifle barrel around. "Whore! Slut!"

"No!" she shrieked. "He made me do it, Harold! Don't kill me, darling! *Shoot him*!"

It was too late for that. Cartwright's finger was already squeezing the trigger. Tom's hand grabbed for his revolver frantically as he realized that his plan had gone awry—that the banker was about to shoot his wife.

There wasn't a sound in the room as the firing pin slammed home, hitting on an empty shell casing. Stunned when the rifle didn't fire, Cartwright stared down at the rifle, shaking his head in disbelief.

Tom realized that Cartwright had failed to clear the chamber from his first shot by levering another round into the rifle. How long would it take him to rectify his mistake? he wondered. The revolver was already in his hands, the hammer cocked, ready to fire. Tom forced himself to lay the gun on the nightstand again.

"You'd still rather face a woman than a man,

wouldn't you, Cartwright?" Tom taunted, praying that the banker would return to his original target. "Come on, you spineless coward! Put another round into that rifle and see if you've got guts enough to shoot me!"

Wild-eyed, Harold Cartwright spun around, pulling at the gun, sending the spent cartridge thudding out onto the floor as he reloaded.

"Bastard!" he screamed, bringing the rifle up, his finger contracting. "I'll show you who's a goddamned coward!"

It seemed like an eternity to Tom as he watched the wavering gun barrel. Still, he made no move to reach his own weapon. Slowly he brought his left hand up to his forehead, his trembling fingers running along the crease of scar tissue there, massaging it gently as he watched the banker's eyes for the signal he knew would come.

Cartwright's eyes told Tom he was about to be shot a split-second before the banker's finger could pull the trigger of the rifle. The roar of the gun came just as Tom rolled to his right. The bullet plowed harmlessly into the spot where he had just been, passing through the soft pillow and continuing on through the frame wall.

Cartwright saw Tom leap off the bed and crash against the nightstand. There was no hesitation this time as he reloaded and swung the gun down on his target, squeezing off another shot.

The bullet hit Tom a few inches below and just to the left of his shoulder, slicing through the flesh and shattering the bone with a force that sent him slamming backwards. A fiery inferno of pain filled Tom's whole upper body as he saw the gaping wound flooding with blood and bits of bone splinter.

He could hear screaming—his own and Amy's, and for a moment he thought he was going to lose consciousness. Desperately he tried to shake off the pain and dizziness as his fingers fought to keep control of the gun in his right hand. *It's no use*, he thought, *I can't hold it . . . I can't . . .*

He could see the banker coming closer now, reloading as he crossed the few feet of carpeted floor that separated them. There was a triumphant smile on Cartwright's face when the rifle came up again—this time pointed directly at Tom's head.

"You scum!" Cartwright screamed down at him, flecks of his heated saliva landing on Tom's face. "You'll never take another man's woman, by Christ!"

Tom had no idea how he managed to get his hand working, how he could pull such a terrible weight as the Colt revolver up. It was as if someone else was guiding him, using their strength in place of his own.

There was another roar, and then a low, gutteral, animal-like squeal as Tom's bullet caught Harold Cartwright in the stomach. The banker didn't go down at once. He stood there, swaying back and forth on his feet, a stunned expression on his tortured features. The rifle was still in his hands, the finger still poised a fraction of an inch from the cold steel of the trigger.

Then, with a soft moan, the banker's lips opened and a stream of scarlet blood began flowing out of the corner. And he came down, folding like a discarded piece of clothing. Then he died.

And all Tom could hear were screams and loud voices and the sound of people crowding into the room. Before he lost consciousness he tried desperately to pick out the face of Amy Cartwright, but it was no use.

Tom came to that afternoon in the small clinic behind Doctor Mayberry's office. His eyes opened slowly, trying to focus, as the terrible pain in his shoulder came back. He moaned, feeling nauseous from the pulsating agony.

"How do you feel, son?" Miles Townsend asked.

"Not good," Tom replied weakly, his voice barely a hoarse whisper. "What happened?"

"You were a goddamned fool, letting Harold Cartwright get in two shots like that," Townsend replied, shaking his head sadly. "It's a wonder he didn't finish you off instead of just screwing up your shoulder. You're lucky to be alive, son."

"Is he . . . is he dead?"

"Yes, you killed him. There'll be an inquest, of course, but there isn't much question that it was self defense on your part."

"And Amy? Was she hurt?"

"No, just in a state of shock. Doc is going to send her down to the new hospital at Prescott as soon as she can travel, then she'll be going back to her folks in Chicago, I suppose. A pretty young widow like Amy won't have any trouble finding a husband more to her liking . . . not with all of Cartwright's money to see her through."

"Did she tell you about that conversation between her husband and Marcus Owens she overheard?" Tom asked.

"Yes, that clears your brother's name, if it's any consolation to you."

Consolation? Tom thought bitterly. Will it bring Billy back? Or Amos Wicklund? Or, would it erase from his own mind the memory of Amy Cartwright's brutal words about Maria Gomez and Billy? Tom would never forget the way she had huddled hysterically in the corner of the hotel room, afraid for her own life, pleading with her crazed husband to shoot Tom instead of her.

"What about the others? Jim Conroy and his men?"

"The old man and eight of his hands are dead. The boy and the others are in custody. They'll stand trial for lynching Billy, I'd guess." He paused, reaching into his pocket. He handed Tom the familiar badge of authority Tom had worn for so many years. "Amos Wicklund told me you'd given this to him for safekeeping," Miles said. "I found it in his things. You'll be wanting it back now, won't you?"

Tom nodded, feeling weak and faint.

"I will," he said simply. "I've felt mighty bare without it hanging on my shirt. You haven't mentioned Jeb Fallon, Townsend. As soon as I'm up and fit to ride, I'm going after him."

Townsend sighed.

"Are you fixing to shoot him, too?" he asked, frowning. "If so, you might not find the next lawman as understanding as I've been."

Tom shook his head, holding up the badge.

"I'll use this when I go after him. When I find him . . . well, I'll bring him in for trial and then dance on his goddamned grave when they've hung him!"

"Yes, I believe you will," the lawman said grimly. He got up. "And after that?"

Tom didn't reply for several moments.

"Well, sir, there's a girl down in Whitehorse I met," he said slowly, thinking of Margo. "She's had a bad shake and I'd like to see if I can't help make up for all the troubles she's had." He shrugged. "It may not work out, but you never know."

The deputy sheriff turned to leave when he saw that Tom's eyes had closed in sleep. The shiny badge still lay atop his chest, where it had fallen from his fingers.

That's where it belongs, Miles Townsend thought, looking down at Tom.